MEET ME THERE

A RIDGEWATER HIGH NOVEL

JUDY CORRY

ISBN-13: **978-1986244091**

ISBN-10: **1986244091**

Cover Design by Victorine E. Lieske

Edited by Precy Larkins

ALSO BY JUDY CORRY

For my daughter Janelle

1

ASHLYN

BREAKING *up with Noah was a good thing.* I gave my reflection a pep talk one more time before leaving the locker room. *You made the right choice. Life is better without him.*

I drew in a deep breath, trying to calm my first-day-of-school jitters. My blonde hair looked okay after being in a ponytail for this morning's 6:30 a.m. drill team practice. My blue eyes were maybe a little tired looking, but that was to be expected since I'd slept terribly last night. At least my new outfit rocked—an awesome floral printed blouse with dark skinny jeans. It had felt like Christmas when I'd found the last shirt in my size at Chic Girl Boutique. Being a tall girl made it hard to find shirts that fit my long torso just right.

I inspected myself one last time before pulling my bag over my shoulder and leaving the deserted locker room. All the other drill team girls had left five minutes ago, excited to see everyone again after summer break.

I made it to the top of the stairs that led away from the gym, and then scanned the hall. There were different clusters of students standing around, but no Noah.

Good. I breathed a sigh of relief. Last year, when we were still together, he'd always wait for me in the mornings. It was nice he'd decided to change his routine as well. If I was lucky, I might be able to avoid seeing him all morning. Juniors and seniors didn't usually have many classes together, so if I could figure out a way to avoid him at lunch I wouldn't have to see him at all.

I was walking into the main hall when I saw a poster that made my stomach drop.

No!

I rushed forward and ripped the paper from the wall. There was only one person in this school who would do something like this.

I'm going to kill him. I'm going to kill Luke Davenport.

I stared at the flyer. There was a hand-drawn picture that I assumed was supposed to look like me, since my name stood out in big, bold letters right above it. It looked like a seven-year-old's art project.

BOYFRIEND WANTED

For: Ashlyn Brooks

Junior. 5'8"ish. Dancer. Blonde hair. Blue or Green Eyes. (I think)

He was starting this up again? I shook my head and read over the headline once more. He didn't even do his research before posting the ridiculous thing. I was five-foot-nine and my eyes were most definitely blue. No, I didn't have one green eye and one blue eye like this hideous portrait suggested—something he might notice if he ever took the time to actually look at me instead of pulling these annoying pranks.

But he'd been pulling pranks like this since last spring. It all started when he slipped extra baking soda in my cake during

Foods class—and all because I grabbed the last non-flowery apron, leaving him to look like a field of daisies exploded all over his front. One prank led to another, and before long, we were in a war—a friendly war, anyway. I thought he'd forget about our rivalry over the summer, but apparently, he still had nothing better to do with his time. We'd always kept our pranks fairly harmless, but this...this was going too far. How long had these flyers been up? And how many people had seen them? Had Noah seen them and thought *I* had posted them? I was going to throw up.

I read the rest of the flyer.

Seeking guys with the following qualifications:
Happy to commit. (Good ol' ball and chain.)
Loves to pamper his girl.
Tall, dark, and handsome preferred, but short and squatty are OK.
Must love shopping for hours at Chic Girl Boutique.
Must be fine with watching chick flicks over football.

If interested, call Ashlyn at 315-555-7892
Or wait for me by my black Mercedes after school for your interview.

My jaw dropped. He actually put my real number on there. I crumpled the flyer in a ball and looked down the hall bustling with students. There were identical ads taped on lockers all along the row. My face flushed with heat as I rushed down the tiled floor, knowing I only had a couple of minutes before the bell rang. I didn't want to be late for my first class. I ripped down sign after sign, going down the main hall as fast as I could in three-inch wedges.

The warning bell rang.

No!

I made one mad dash, ripping the last flyer down before the hall was completely full of students rushing to their first-period classes. I threw the offending flyers in the trash and headed to my locker to grab my History notebook.

My friend and next-door neighbor, Eliana, saw me as soon as I turned the corner.

"Did you see them?" Eliana asked in a hushed tone, her blue eyes searching mine for signs of a freak-out.

I nodded. "Just barely. I took down as many as I could on my way here."

"Me too. Your brother and I started yanking them down as soon as we got here, but we could only get the ones in this hall."

I opened my locker, resisting the urge to punch it. "Why does Luke keep doing this? Doesn't he have anyone else he can annoy?"

Eliana leaned her barely five-foot frame against her locker, her notebooks hugged to her chest. Her dad was from Italy and her mom was from here, so she looked gorgeous with her darker features and light eyes. "I have no idea, but we definitely need to get him back good this time."

"For real." He'd taken these pranks to a new level of public humiliation. He needed some public humiliation himself.

My brother Jess walked up behind us then. "Do you want me to take care of Luke this time?" he asked in his protective, older-brother voice.

"No. You don't need to get involved. But I'm open to suggestions for revenge."

Jess checked his watch. "The late bell is gonna ring in a minute, but we'll talk more about this after school." He looked at Eliana. "See you at Math Club?"

She nodded, and then Jess left us.

"You guys have Math Club on the first day of school?"

Eliana shrugged. "Not officially. But since Jess and I are in charge this year, he figured we should go over some stuff with Miss Maloney today if we could."

I couldn't keep a grin from spreading across my cheeks. "You guys are such nerds."

"And proud of it!" She grinned back. "Anyway, I better get to class. But I'll grab any flyers I see on my way. Sorry about this. Luke went overboard this time."

I was almost to my History classroom when I spotted the devil himself. Luke was leaning against the wall as if he'd been waiting for me to walk by. It wouldn't surprise me if he'd stolen my class schedule from the office. When our eyes met, a smirk lifted his lips. He pushed himself off the wall and his long legs fell into step next to mine.

"How's your first day going?" he asked.

"Fabulously," I said, my voice dripping with sarcasm. "Pretty much a dream. I've always wanted to see a cartoon version of my face plastered all over the school. Did you draw that picture yourself?"

He grinned. "No, actually my neighbor was selling her art on the sidewalk last weekend and her picture reminded me so much of you I had to buy it."

I wanted to smack that smug look off his face. How could a guy who looked so cute and innocent be so devious? It wasn't fair. Guys should come with a warning label. I mean, I could've saved myself a lot of trouble last year if Noah's cover had matched his inside.

"It was great to see you again as always, Luke," I said when we reached my destination. "Oh, and my eyes are blue, for future reference."

He stopped and peered into my eyes for a moment, his own brown ones catching me by surprise. Had they always had that much gold mixed in with them?

"Ah, yes, blue," he said, his warm minty breath tickling my face. "I'll have to tell my neighbor so she can get it right next time. You wouldn't happen to know what your blood type is, would you?"

My stomach lurched. "My blood type?"

The smirk was back on his lips. "Totally joking there."

I slugged him in the arm—a very well-defined arm. No wonder he was the football captain this year. He probably worked out in all of his free time to get so sculpted. He definitely hadn't been so big last spring. He seemed taller as well. He had to be at least six-two or six-three.

I shook my head, hoping he hadn't noticed my lingering gaze. He was still rubbing his arm where I'd hit him. That made me smile. Who says dancers aren't tough? "You better hurry to your class before the bell rings. I'll look forward to planning our next meeting."

He raised an eyebrow. "By 'meeting,' you mean your next form of revenge?"

"Of course."

His grin spread wider. For some reason, one I couldn't understand, Luke seemed to be looking forward to my participation in the pranking game again.

Deciding I'd have to figure him out later, I turned on my heel to find my seat in U.S. History.

My phone buzzed in my pocket. There were about a dozen missed text messages and five missed calls, all from numbers I didn't recognize.

315-555-2934: **UR hot. I'll be your boyfriend.**

315-555-2345: **I'll dump my girlfriend 4 you.**

315-555-9723: **meet me in the maintenance closet @ lunch 4 a good time.**

The rest of the texts were along the same lines. Who in their right mind would think I'd be interested in any of those things? Oh yeah, guys who thought the ad was actually real.

I'm going to kill Luke Davenport.

I was barely able to concentrate on my classes the rest of the morning because I kept getting texts. Most of them were from total idiots, but there were a few that seemed sincere. Had every guy at school seen the ads? There couldn't be that many guys interested in dating me. It's not like I was that popular. Maybe Luke put all his friends up to this. I wouldn't put it past him. I mean, no guy in their right mind would actually be interested in filling the "boyfriend wanted" spot, given those outrageous requirements on the flyer.

If my phone was this popular during class, what the heck was I supposed to do during lunch? Jess and Eliana's meeting would probably take forever. And without them, I didn't have anyone else to hang out with since I'd always been with Noah. If I sat at a table by myself, Luke's buddies might try "helping" his plan along even further.

The bell rang, and I fully planned to join Jess and Eliana in their meeting today. I could pretend to be a Mathlete. It might be kind of nice to have built-in tutors everywhere.

I took my time packing up my things from Ceramics. If I waited in here for a few minutes, then I wouldn't have to run into Noah during lunch.

But Noah must have had the same idea because when I stepped out into the hall, I came face to face with my ex for the first time since our breakup. My breath caught in my throat. He looked even better than he had when we were dating. And not seeing him in two months hadn't changed anything about my body's reaction to him. He still had the same dark brooding brown eyes and auburn hair with a slight curl in it.

He seemed to take in my appearance as well, and I couldn't help but wonder what he thought about seeing me again.

"Saw your boyfriend-wanted posters this morning," he said in his deep, gravelly voice. "Having a hard time getting along without me?"

I flushed, my brain scrambling for a response. "I didn't put those flyers up."

He crossed his arms and chuckled. "Yeah, well, if anybody tries to fill the ad, I'll tell them not to waste their time."

My eyes instantly burned at his words and the memories they evoked. I had put up with so much while we dated, and now I was a waste of time?

I pinched my eyes shut and sucked in a quick breath, willing the tears to stay inside. I couldn't let Noah know his words had any effect on me. He didn't deserve to have that kind of power over me anymore.

"Goodbye, Noah." I whirled around and walked away, knowing I wouldn't be able to keep the tears at bay for much longer.

"See ya."

While Luke Davenport was mostly annoying, Noah Taylor was the bad habit I'd broken too late.

2

LUKE

"THANK YOU, Mr. Sawyer, for never locking this room," I whispered under my breath as I slipped into the dark Chemistry lab and sat down on the floor beside the door. I felt like a coward hiding in here during lunch, but I was going to explode if one more stranger came up and told me how sorry they were to hear about my mom dying this summer. Sure, posting those "boyfriend wanted" posters for Ashlyn had distracted everyone for a while, but apparently, our school counselor thought I was "acting out." And to help me "grieve" in a more appropriate way, she had rallied a committee of do-gooders to try and cheer me up.

But I didn't need a bunch of girls looking at me with their sad, pitying eyes, trying to get me to talk about my "feelings." These pranks had been awesome last year when my mom was sick, why shouldn't they help me now?

My stomach growled, reminding me it was there. I smothered it with my arms.

Just a few more minutes and I could sneak out to my Jeep to grab some lunch.

I was about to stand when the door opened, and someone tripped over my sprawled legs.

Oof!

"Sorry!" a female voice squealed as she landed on me.

A girl? Had one of those do-gooders followed me here? How many people had the school counselor told?

I tried to help the girl get up, but it was so dark and there were no windows here—our heads crashed together instead.

"Ouch!" she said.

"Sorry." I rubbed my forehead where our skulls had collided.

We righted ourselves, and I leaned back against the wall of cupboards behind us. She scooted a few feet away.

We sat in silence for a few moments until I heard her sniffling like she was trying not to cry.

"Are you okay? Did my head hurt you?" She sniffled again, so I asked, "Are you crying?"

"No," she said, her voice uneven. "I'm just hiding from a stupid jerk."

There was something familiar about her voice.

I couldn't have everyone at school knowing the football captain hid in the Chemistry lab during lunch, so I lowered my voice, just in case this was someone I knew. "Who's the jerk?"

Okay, it sounded like I had a bad cold, but hopefully, I hadn't said enough earlier for her to notice the difference. Was it too late to start using my fake British accent? I was excellent at impersonations. Random talent, but it did come in handy sometimes.

"Nobody important," she said.

Okay, so some dude made her cry. She probably wouldn't want to be in the same room as me after hearing what I'd done that morning. Luckily for me though, Ashlyn hadn't cried. She was too mad to do that. Boy, was I going to be in trouble once she figured out how to get me back. She always came back with something strong.

"If it makes you feel better, I think he's a jerk too." I tried to make it sound like I was joking, but somehow my fake British accent slipped out when I said those words. Oh well, not like it mattered. We were sitting in the dark, and I'd be leaving soon anyway.

She laughed, and I felt like I'd been hit by a sack of rocks. I knew that laugh. I'd heard that sweet melodic sound about a billion times last year in Foods class.

This girl was Ashlyn Brooks.

Crap! My stomach shrunk in on itself. Had she been crying because of my prank this morning? She'd seemed fine when I talked to her. Maybe her tears were because of my friends' texts? I'd told them to keep it clean—to just have fun with her. But I should have realized that was impossible. Kellen and Jake had a few too many concussions to follow my directions very well.

"You don't even know which jerk I'm talking about." She laughed again.

Oh, but I did. She was talking about me. I needed to get out of there before she figured out who I was. I snuck a peek in her direction and was grateful I could barely make out her silhouette. If I couldn't pick out much about her, then hopefully she couldn't see much of me. I moved my leg closer to the sliver of light coming from under the door, just in case.

"Sorry about tripping over you," she said like she still had no idea who I was.

I cleared my throat and focused on maintaining my British accent. "Sorry about blocking the door." *Okay, Luke, it's time to leave now. You're pushing your luck every second you stay in here.*

But my legs seemed to be frozen to the tiled floor. Plus, if I did leave, I'd have to open the door and the light would give away who I was. And then she would hate me even more for disguising my voice. So I sat there.

"Are you from England or something?"

Definitely *or something.* "Uh, yeah. I moved here over the summer."

"What part of England?" she asked like she thought it was so cool. Or hot. My ex-girlfriend always said my impression of a British guy was sexy.

"I'm from London."

"That's so cool! I've always wanted to visit."

"You should. It's nice...and overcast?" *You're an idiot, Luke.* I needed to stop pretending like I knew anything about England when the extent of my knowledge came from the *Pride and Prejudice*-type movies my mom had me watch with her when she was sick.

"Is it weird that I want to sit in the dark for a while longer?" she asked.

"Depends."

"Depends on what?"

"Depends on whether you think it's weird that I want to stay in here too." Which was so strange because it was true. Ashlyn and I were supposed to be sworn rivals.

She laughed. Maybe that was a good sign? I heard her shift on the tile floor like she was getting comfortable.

"What were you doing sitting here in the dark anyway?" she asked.

I bit my lip, trying to decide if I wanted to tell her the truth or not. There was something about the anonymity that made me feel like I could tell her anything. Here in the dark, I could be anyone.

I could be myself.

Or at least my real self who also happened to have a British accent and a really deep voice.

"I was hiding," I said.

"Hiding from who?"

Reality.

I shook my head. "Doesn't matter. I just need to lay low for a few minutes."

"Looks like neither one of us wants to say much about why we're in here," she said. "I guess I better get going anyway."

"Wait!" I said, surprising myself.

She seemed to startle. "Why?"

"Because I-I still don't know anything about you," I lied. Why was I doing this? I should be relieved she wanted to go, not suddenly interested in getting to know Ashlyn better.

I expected her to stand. But she didn't. "What do you want to know?" she asked in a soft voice.

I thought about it. "Hmmm. It's kind of fun not knowing who I'm talking to, so let's set up some rules."

"Rules?"

I smiled, though I knew she couldn't see it. "Yes, rules. This is likely the only opportunity we'll ever have to get to know someone without seeing them first. It's like the ultimate clean slate, aside from the fact that I know you're a girl, and you know I'm a guy."

"And that you're from England."

Right.

I continued, "We should make a rule that we can only speak the truth in here. No saying something just because we think that's what people want to hear. Wouldn't it be nice to get to know someone with all the walls down?" The irony of my whole honesty comment was not lost on me as I used my fake accent.

She was quiet for a moment. Then she said, "That would be nice. There're no pre-judgments based on looks, reputation, or anything. We can get to know the real us." I heard a smile in her voice. "I kind of like that idea."

"Good." I found myself smiling as well. "So, tell me about yourself, Mystery Girl. Tell me things you don't tell anyone else."

"Mystery Girl?" She laughed. "I'm not that interesting."

"Oh, but you are. I'm already intrigued." What could Ashlyn Brooks darkest secrets be?

She laughed again. "Are we talking surface-level stuff or deep stuff?"

"I'm tired of the surface level. That's all anyone wants to hear these days. Let's go scuba diving."

"Scuba diving?" Her voice was covered in disbelief. "Are you sure?"

"Definitely."

"Okay, you asked for it," she said in a low voice. She was quiet for a long time, but then she let out a tiny giggle. "I really, really like the color blue. Like, every time I'm outside I look at the sky and sigh."

What? "Are you for real?"

It sounded like her shoulders were shaking against the cupboards, almost as if she was suppressing her laughter. "Sorry, I had to. Things were way too serious in here."

I shook my head and smiled at this version of Ashlyn that I'd never known was there.

"How about I go first then," I said. But as soon as I said that, I had nothing interesting to say. Nothing that would fit this *all-important moment* of finally letting someone know who Luke Davenport was beneath all the layers and masks...and fake accents.

"It's harder than you thought, huh?" she said, seeming to understand my hesitation.

"Yeah." I sighed. "The only thing I could come up with was that my favorite food is pizza."

More laughter from her. *Score!* Maybe scuba diving wasn't that important anyway. She'd been on the verge of crying when she first came in here...because of me...and now she was laughing...also because of me. If anything, that made this interaction a success.

Her phone buzzed from inside her bag, and she pulled it out. The screen lit up, which let me see her profile better: Perfectly straight nose. Full lips. Dainty chin. Yep, it was definitely Ashlyn.

She groaned, and then said, "I better go. Maybe we should try telling our deepest darkest secrets again sometime."

My breath caught in my throat. Really? She wanted to meet me again? "Yeah, that would be cool. Wanna try again tomorrow? Same time, same place, same lighting?" My pulse throbbed as I waited for her to respond. Who knew the possibility of being rejected by Ashlyn could be so scary?

"I can't tomorrow, but how about Monday?" she said to my relief.

"Monday would be great."

"Okay, I really do need to leave now. Promise you won't look?" she asked.

I smiled. "I'll even wait a few minutes before I come out, for good measure."

She stood, and I moved my legs out of the way so she wouldn't trip over them again. I heard her hand fumbling around before she opened the door. When the light from the hallway poured in, I lifted my backpack in front of my face in case she glanced back.

The door shut behind her and the room was dark again.

I sighed, leaning my head against the cupboard. I had no idea what I was doing, or if I could even keep this fake British guy act up, but I hoped she'd come back, because that was the first real conversation I'd had since my mom died.

3

ASHLYN

AFTER SCHOOL, in the parking lot, several guys surrounded my car. From seniors and all the way down to freshmen, though most of them were Luke's friends from the football team.

Luke's best friend, Kellen Berkey, was leaning against my door. "You didn't respond to my text, so I'm here for my interview."

"Sorry, which message was yours? My phone has been busier than normal for some reason."

"I'm the 'Call Me for a Good Time' guy."

Gag. Yeah, no. "And you can't imagine why I didn't respond?"

He shrugged. "It usually works for me."

I rolled my eyes and pushed past him. "Not interested."

His best friend, Jake Haley, sidled up to me then. "What about me? I waited in the maintenance closet all during lunch."

My heart jolted at that. I thought I'd been in the Chemistry lab, but was it possible I'd been wrong? Jake couldn't have been the British guy I'd talked to, could he? I'd been listening for a British accent all afternoon but hadn't heard one yet. Could Jake have pretended to be from England to try to romance me since he knew all girls thought accents were hot?

"Did anyone show up?" I had to ask him, just in case. Jake *was* pretty cute after all, even if his choice of texts left something to be desired.

"No. And I missed part of my next class because I was still waiting for you."

Okay, good. I really had talked to a British guy with a deep voice that made me want to sigh.

I shook thoughts of my lunchtime experience away. "Don't blame your tardiness on me. Maybe you should have written a more compelling text message."

"Nah, if you don't like my style it wouldn't have worked out between us." He elbowed his friend on the side. "We better get going to football practice anyway. Can't have you making me late for that too."

Kellen and Jake left with the rest of their football buddies, leaving me behind with just one more guy standing in the way of me escaping into my car.

I didn't recognize this boy. He might have been a freshman, standing about two inches shorter than me. Probably hadn't met his growth spurt yet.

He eyed me nervously, looking like he was about to puke. "I— I saw your flyers this morning. You might have missed my text. I'm the one who asked if you wanted to go to the skate park this weekend with me. It could be a lot of fun."

My heart went out to him. While the other guys had been joking around, this guy was sincere.

But I wasn't ready to date again, so I said, "That's really sweet, but I'm actually taking a break from dating. I just broke up with my boyfriend over the summer, and I need to work on myself for a while."

The boy looked down at his shoes and nodded. "I understand. I figured it was a long shot anyway."

He left me, and I escaped into my car. I sighed and leaned back into the leather seat, locking the doors, just in case. I was so going to kill Luke Davenport.

As I pulled my car out of its parking spot, I noticed Luke standing beside his Sahara Orange Jeep Wrangler with his football bag slung over his shoulder. He slipped his smirky smile onto his face when our eyes met. I really needed to think of a good way to get him back.

THURSDAYS WERE MY LONGEST DAYS. I started off the morning with drill team practice at six-thirty a.m., went to school all day, and then had to go back for our evening drill practice from five to eight. I was starving by the time I got home.

I parked my car in my garage and headed into our two-story Tudor-style house. My parents had fully gutted and renovated our home ten years ago while we spent the summer in Martha's Vineyard, so even though it was over a hundred years old, it was like a brand-new house inside.

The warm smell of my mom's favorite vanilla-scented candle greeted my nose once I stepped into the mudroom. I hung my keys on a hook by the door then went down the hall to see what I could scrounge up for dinner. Mom was standing in the kitchen in her red Louis Vuitton's, with her blonde hair pulled back in a bun, wiping invisible dust off the cupboard doors. I checked the clock on the wall. Eight-ten p.m. Yep, she was right on schedule with her evening routine.

She puffed a piece of hair out of her eyes and glanced back at me as she rinsed off her dust rag. "I left a container of salad for you in the fridge."

Yay, salad. Again. My mom was a health nut, so salads were an everyday occurrence around our house. If I didn't have one for lunch, I could count on getting one for dinner. But at least she let me have dressing on mine. She was crazy and always ate hers without it.

I grabbed the container of salad, thanked my mom, and went upstairs to my bedroom to eat while I finished my U.S. History assignment. I dropped my drill bag onto my queen-sized bed then sat down at my desk with my dinner and books.

An hour later, I was putting my notebook away when my phone pinged.

I groaned. That better not be another guy pretending to be interested in dating me.

Eliana: **Do you still want to plan your revenge on Luke tonight?**

Me: **Just finished my homework so come on over!**

My phone's battery was almost dead, so I plugged it into the charger on my antique-white nightstand, and then sat on my bed to wait for Eliana to walk over from her house next door.

"Is Eliana coming over tonight?" Jess said, knocking on my bedroom door. He must have just gotten home from his study date with his latest girlfriend, Stacy. Or was Stacy last week's girlfriend? I shook my head. Keeping up with my brother's dating schedule was too time-consuming. Though it did pay well—Eliana and I had a betting addiction, trying to guess how long each of Jess's relationships would last. I usually won.

"She's actually on her way right now. We're gonna make plans for tomorrow. I'm thinking we should do something to humiliate Luke at the game."

Jess grinned and leaned against the door frame. "I have the best idea."

"That's what you said last time. And no, filling his locker with teddy bears was lame. I think he actually liked that one, with how he carried the big fluffy brown one around all day."

"No, this one is really good. I promise."

Eliana stepped up behind Jess then. "Hey, guys."

"Come on in." I patted a spot on my pink-and-gold comforter for her to sit down. "Jess just told me he has the most amazing idea for tomorrow's prank."

Eliana smiled at Jess. "You aren't thinking about putting stuffed penguins in his locker this time, are you?"

Jess blushed—he'd been doing that a lot more around Eliana lately. "No, I was thinking we could put some Icy Hot in his jock-strap before the big game tomorrow."

"Luke's jockstrap. Eww!" I made a face. "Even if that's not the grossest prank ever, how would I even get the Icy Hot in there? I'm pretty sure he'd notice me standing behind him, and there's no way I'm going into the boy's locker room."

"We'll have to do it when he's not around," Jess said as if it was obvious. "I'm pretty sure he leaves his Jeep unlocked, with his football bag in the backseat. We could get to it during the pep rally tomorrow."

I bit my lip. As disgusting as it was, it did sound like an awesome way to get Luke back. And he needed payback for what he'd done that morning.

"Okay, let's do it!" I said. "We might as well give the football fans a good show for their opening game."

Jess's phone rang in his pocket. He pulled it out, checked the screen, and groaned. "It's Stacy."

"And why is that a problem?" Shouldn't he be excited that his girlfriend was calling him?

"She wants me to go to some play tomorrow night instead of the football game. I'm gonna have to tell her I'm going to the game with you guys, and then she's gonna tell me how I should put her needs first."

"Well, maybe that's a sign that she's not for you after all. It's only been a week, and most couples stay in the 'my girlfriend is the best' stage for at least a month." It would be amazing if he ever made it that long. Seriously, a gallon of milk left on the counter would probably stay good longer than Jess's relationships.

"You're just saying that so you can win your bet with Eliana."

I grinned. "Maybe. But it's still true regardless."

"And how many days did you bet this one would last?" Jess asked Eliana.

"Fourteen." She peeked up at him with a guilty look.

Jess's expression sank. "So I guess you don't have *that* much more faith in me than my sister."

Eliana shrugged. "I was just being realistic."

"I'll prove you both wrong. In fact, I'll tell Stacy I'd love to go to the play on Saturday instead, since I have special plans for us at the game. This way both of us will get what we want. I mean, Stacy is pretty cool most of the time."

He played with his phone for a moment to call her back, walking down the hall to his bedroom.

"My brother has issues," I said to Eliana.

"Yes, but that's why we love him so much." She smiled. "At least he keeps his love life fresh and exciting. I'm definitely not one to pretend I'm an expert in love."

"Too bad Ryan Miller had to move away last summer, huh?" I grinned. Eliana had been in love with Jess's buddy, Ryan, for years.

"Yeah, well. It was pretty hopeless anyway, since he barely noticed me the four years he lived here. It's probably time for me to find a new crush. Too bad the guys at our school don't even realize I'm alive."

I was pretty sure my brother noticed her, in more than the "we're just best friends" kind of way, but Eliana was somehow still blind to it. She had no idea that his string of girlfriends had nothing to do with the actual girl, and everything to do with the fact that they weren't his best friend: Eliana.

Instead of saying anything about my brother, I shrugged and said, "If you're serious about finding a new crush, I have a whole list of guys looking for a girlfriend on my phone. Maybe we should text them back." I laughed.

Eliana pushed some of her dark hair behind her ear. "How did your interviews go after school, anyway? Were there tons of guys hanging around your car?"

I rolled my eyes. "I'm pretty sure Luke put the whole football team up to it. Though I did have a little freshman boy waiting for me too. I felt horrible saying no to him."

"Oh, sad." Eliana frowned.

"Tell me about it."

"So, you aren't interested in any of the guys you talked to today?"

The memory of the British guy in the Chemistry lab came to my mind. "There might be one guy."

She sat up straighter, suddenly animated. "Really? Who?"

"I actually don't know."

"How can you not know? Did he just send a bunch of mysterious texts or something?"

"No. We bumped into each other in the Chem lab during lunch."

I told her all about tripping over the guy in the dark and how we had just sat in there for a while.

"I was kind of crying because Noah was a jerk, as usual, but this new guy from England was so nice. Most guys run in the opposite direction when a girl is crying, but he stayed and made me laugh again. He actually wanted to get to know me better, unlike most other guys at school."

"Stupid Noah. But I'm glad this guy was nice and not some sort of Chem lab creeper."

"He actually asked me to meet with him again."

"He did?" Nervousness crept into her eyes. "Are you sure that's a good idea? This guy could be anybody, really. It could have been Janitor Earl for all you know."

"Gross!" My 'creeper radar' hadn't gone off once during our whole exchange...and I had a pretty good creeper radar. But her comment did make me think. "I think this guy's fine. Don't they make guys more gentlemanly in England anyway?"

"I think they just sound more gentlemanly." Eliana laughed. "I'm pretty sure guys are the same everywhere. There are always good guys and bad guys."

"Do you know of any new British guys at school?" I asked.

She shook her head. "Can't think of any. And I'm sure I would have noticed a British accent. Pretty sure all the girls would be talking about him, too. But it's a big school. So who knows."

I thought about it. "Maybe he's just quiet. He *was* hiding in the Chem lab."

A sad thought came over me. Maybe this British guy didn't have any friends and planned to spend every lunch period hiding in that dark room. He had wanted to meet tomorrow at lunch. Was he just so lonely that he was desperate for any sort of company?

"Are you gonna meet up with him again?" Eliana interrupted my thoughts.

I had to. I needed to show my new countryman that the people in Ridgewater, New York were just as nice as the people in London, England. We'd become friends, and maybe he'd feel comfortable enough at school to make friends when he wasn't in the dark.

"I'm gonna go back to find out more about him. Who knows, maybe he won't even show up." But I hoped he would.

4

LUKE

FOOTBALL PRACTICE SUCKED. Coach Hobbs was having a bad day and decided to take it out on us by making us run ladders until we all collapsed. And to top off my night, I remembered I still hadn't washed my laundry since Coach issued us our uniforms, which meant it stank like butt. So, instead of leaving my bag in the Jeep tonight, I had to haul it back in the house and do a freaking load of laundry. Lame.

I opened the front door to my family's two-story brick house and stepped into the tiled entryway. "I'm home," I called out of habit. No one answered. Of course, no one answered. No one was here anymore. And my dad was probably working late just like he'd been doing almost every night since July fifth.

I strode into the laundry room and emptied my football bag into the front-loading washing machine. Once the load had started, I heated up a frozen burrito for dinner, smothered it with salsa and sour cream, and sat at the kitchen island.

Don't forget your veggies, my mom's voice sounded in my head. I sighed and grabbed a cucumber from the fridge, biting into it with the crunch.

I followed my meal with a cold glass of milk then headed to my room to do my homework. I hated how quiet the house was now. My brother, Alec, was in the Army, and now that my mom was gone, my dad didn't think he needed to be home anymore. Or at least that's how it seemed. I knew he was just trying to cope with our loss, but still.

My Psychology assignment didn't take long. I checked the time on my phone. It was only eight-fifteen p.m. Definitely too early to go to sleep. I texted Kellen and Jake to see what they were up to.

Kellen: **Got stuck picking up my sister from soccer.**

Jake: **Can't hang out. Maren's coming over tonight. ;)**

I sighed and pulled out my laptop. Looks like I'd have plenty of time to figure out my next prank for Ashlyn. But instead of looking online for ideas, I found myself researching things about England. I didn't even know if I wanted to go back to the Chemistry lab on Monday. Sure, the idea of talking to someone without them knowing who I was sounded awesome and all, but did I really want to talk to Ashlyn? I mean, she was okay to look at. I'd probably admit that she was hot if forced, but she was also annoying. I probably wouldn't go back after all. Standing her up would be a great prank...even if she didn't know it was me.

But I looked up popular British-English phrases anyway. If I did go back, I could just throw in a "brilliant" or "tea and crumpets" into the conversation and she'd never even know the difference. In fact, pretending to be some British dude would be an awesome prank in and of itself.

A huge grin stretched across my face. She'd have her revenge ready for me by Monday, so it would be perfect to pretend to be some understanding, gentlemanly guy that she felt she could trust. All I would need is some juicy information, and then I'd flip on the lights and tell her it was all fake. That would be awesome.

I closed my laptop and switched on the lamp. The sun was starting to set, and I hated what it did to the lighting in my room. Ever since my mom died, I couldn't stand twilight. There was something about the dim lighting that made me feel like I was going crazy. I put on some music, hoping it would help, and then I made my way back to the laundry room, turning on lights the whole way there.

GAME DAY. Ridgewater High vs. Homer High. I grabbed an early dinner and drove back to the school to warm up for the game. I pulled my football bag over my shoulder and made my way toward the locker room. The drill team was practicing their dance for tonight's halftime show. Ashlyn was in the front row, dancing to the beat of the music. When our eyes met, she smiled. If I didn't know any better, I'd think she was happy to see me, though I couldn't imagine why. The only thing I could think of was that she might have found a way to put something in my locker to embarrass me. Hopefully, it wasn't any more teddy bears. I had enough of those to last me a lifetime.

But when I opened my locker, all that was in there were my stinky P.E. clothes. Yeah, I should probably take those home and wash them, too.

I dropped my duffel bag by my locker then took a stroll around the room, passing through a maze of my teammates wearing differing amounts of clothing. But I didn't see anything out of the ordinary. Maybe Ashlyn's smile had just been that, a smile. Hopefully, she hadn't somehow figured out it had been me in the Chemistry lab.

I went back to my blue-and-white bag and unzipped it. It

smelled like peppermint. Did Dad switch detergent brands? Probably. He never had to do laundry before, so he most likely didn't even know what kind of soap Mom usually bought.

"You psyched?" Kellen clapped me on the shoulder after I stripped off my shirt.

"Sure. Should be fun, if not for their linebacker. Have you seen him? He's like Bigfoot's cousin." I'd lifted weights all summer to get my mind off my mom, but this guy had to be using steroids or something because he was huge.

"Dude, you're not our captain for nothing. So stop worrying about it like a little old lady."

Coach Hobbs yelled for everyone to get on the field, so I hurried to put on the rest of my uniform. About thirty seconds into my run out to the field, it felt like my crotch was on fire. It took everything I had in me not to scream! I turned around to go back to the locker room. I had to get in the shower immediately. Something bad was happening. Was this some sort of allergic reaction to the new peppermint detergent my dad bought?

"Turn around and get on the field, Davenport!" Coach yelled when I passed him on my way back to the locker room. "Get your butt out there now or you won't be starting tonight!"

"WHAT'S WITH THE DANCING, DUDE?" Jake called to me as we passed the football back and forth along the thirty-yard line. "Drink too much before practice?"

I shook my head. If I said anything it would probably come out sounding like a strangled kitten. But the jumping and stomping around were helping. Maybe not so much with the pain, but at least it was distracting me from it. "Running passes?" I suggested to Jake, managing not to squeak the words out and retain whatever dignity I had left.

Plus, jogging around had to help. The bleachers were already half full, so moving across the field would be less humiliating than having everyone think I was like some kid doing the potty dance.

Running around did help, and after a few minutes, the burning sensation turned into more of a cooling sensation. Maybe I wasn't going to die after all. I could handle this. It was like wearing jock itch powder, just with a bit more of a burn. It was manageable...but still, the first thing I was going to do when I got home was throw that detergent in the trash.

I peeked across the track. The bleachers were almost full now, and a few of the cheerleaders pointed at me while talking to each other. *Great.* I looked down, just to make sure I didn't have something visible going on. Nope, my blue football pants were still blue, and they hadn't started smoking yet.

Coach gave us one final pep talk. As soon as he was done, I ran off toward the locker room to make sure I didn't have some gnarly rash.

The drill team was just coming out of the school when I got there. I waited by the door as they all exited, bouncing on my heels as they took their pretty time coming out the doors.

"Something wrong?" a female voice came from behind me.

Ashlyn.

I didn't have time for her and whatever prank she planned to play on me. I needed to make sure everything was okay down there.

She stepped closer, lifting her face to scrutinize mine. "You're not looking good, Luke. Do you need me to help you with something?"

"I'm fine. Just need to take a leak," I lied. *Hurry up, drill team.* How many girls did we need dancing during halftime anyway?

"Well, good luck on the game tonight," Ashlyn said. "I just

love watching you guys on the field. You all look so *hot* in your uniforms. Or is it more icy than hot?"

I stopped my ridiculous bouncing as my heart stuttered to a halt. This wasn't some allergic reaction to peppermint detergent. Ashlyn had done this to me. Suddenly, it all made sense. The wave and smile in the gym, the smell of peppermint coming from my athletic bag that hadn't been there last night. Ashlyn must have gotten into my things somehow and put Icy Hot on my jock strap.

Suddenly, getting Ashlyn to talk to a fake British guy wasn't nearly bad enough. I needed to make it hurt like I was hurting right now. Oh, yes, I would definitely go back to that room and pretend to be some dreamy guy from England, but I would take it one step further. I would use that deep voice and fake accent for all it was worth. I would talk to Ashlyn, tell her everything she wanted to hear and get her to tell me things she'd never tell anyone else. I'd make her fall in love with me. And then, I would find a way to humiliate her in front of everyone. I'd get her in front of the whole school and tell everyone that I'd just pulled off the biggest prank of all time. Ashlyn would regret the day she messed with Luke Davenport because once I was done with her, her cheeks would be burning way hotter than this Icy Hot ever could.

It was on!

5

ASHLYN

I COULDN'T KEEP from smiling about my prank all weekend. Finally, I had been able to get Luke back the way he deserved. It had been spectacular sneaking out for a moment to watch him dance around the field like he was on fire. Just seeing that with my own two eyes was awesome enough, but then the look on his face when he realized it was me was priceless. I'd totally consider digging through his gym bag again if it meant seeing him go into shock.

But now the ball was back in his court, and I'd be lying if I didn't say I was nervous about him getting me back.

I made it through the first two periods without running into Luke, but it was only inevitable that I'd bump into him before long.

But I couldn't worry about that right now, because I'd be meeting with British Boy in a few minutes. When I wasn't laughing about my prank, I was daydreaming about what today might bring in the Chemistry lab. Would he be there again? And would he still be just as sweet and understanding as he'd been the first day?

I hoped he would, because I definitely wouldn't mind listening to that accent again. Because that accent was way better in person than it was when I watched my old-fashioned English romance movies at home.

The halls finally emptied as students headed to the cafeteria. I was just grabbing the lunch I'd packed for today when Luke turned the corner. He startled when he saw me standing alone in the hall.

I bit my lip to keep my mouth from hanging open. His red V-neck fit his muscular physique perfectly—he looked hot...and not in the Icy Hot kind of way.

I shook my head and blinked my eyes to get those thoughts out of my head. Luke was an annoying jerk who found joy in making my life miserable. He may *look* good, but he wasn't *good.*

He sauntered up next to me, the startled look gone from his face. "What you got in there?" He nodded at my pink lunch box. It seemed like a friendly-enough question, but I needed to keep my guard up. He could attack with revenge at any moment.

"It's my tarantula collection," I said, pulling something off the top of my head. "I was hoping to put them in your locker today, but since you haven't gotten me back yet after my epic prank, I guess they'll have to wait."

Luke leaned against the locker next to mine and gave me one of his heart-stopping smiles. "Trick's on you Ashlyn because my brother and I had tarantulas for pets growing up."

"Seriously?" I raised an eyebrow.

"Seriously."

"Good to know." I shut my locker, hoping he'd get the hint that he could leave now. I needed to get to the Chemistry lab soon or British Boy would think I was standing him up.

But he didn't leave. Instead, he asked, "Where are you headed? I was thinking it might be time for me to admit defeat and call a truce after all."

"Really? Giving up so soon?" I searched his face for a sign that he was lying. And while his mouth didn't slip into the half smile I expected, there was something in his eyes that told me not to trust him.

"To prove I'm sincere, I want to have lunch with you today. It was rude of me to post those flyers. If I'd known you'd broken up with Noah over the summer, I would have picked something different."

Yeah, right. Noah was on the football team with him, so there was about zero chance that it hadn't come up during football camp. In fact, they'd probably planned it together since they were so much the same: conniving and mean. But whatever—I'd gotten my revenge, and oh it was so sweet.

"I already have plans for lunch, so even if I didn't think you were planning to put something nasty in my food, I couldn't go anyway."

"Oh? What are your plans?"

"Um..." My mind scrambled for something to say. There was no way I could let him find out that I was meeting a stranger in the Chemistry lab. He'd for sure find a way to use that information against me. "I have a, um...I just need to get help from Mr. Phipps. I was confused about something in History today."

"I'll walk you there then. It's the least I can do to show you that I have no hard feelings over the way you burned my crotch at the game." He smiled, and this time there was totally something devious in it. Oh, he definitely had hard feelings still.

"You go ahead and get your lunch. I'm fine walking there myself."

But he kept pace with me, and that smirk was still on his face. Had he set up some sort of prank in the hall and was just waiting for me to walk into it?

My heart started pounding as we turned a corner, and I braced myself for *something*. But the hall was empty. Just a wall of lockers and a flickering fluorescent light. I peeked at Luke as he walked beside me. He was as calm as could be. We were almost to Mr. Phipps' door with a poster of Abe Lincoln on it when I stopped in my tracks.

"Actually, I drank a ton of water this morning, so I need to hit the bathroom first. Thanks for walking me here." And I dashed away before he could stop me.

Once I was in the bathroom, I set my lunchbox on the counter and unzipped the lid. Inside sat the scarf I'd packed just in case. I wrapped it loosely around my neck and slung my lunchbox back over my shoulder. After ensuring Luke was nowhere in sight, I snuck out of the bathroom.

I strode past a couple of band nerds who were making out like they thought each other's lips were lunch. I sighed with relief when I made it to the Chemistry lab without running into Luke again. Hopefully, British Boy hadn't left yet.

I TIPTOED up to the door and opened it just a sliver of the way. "Psst. Are you in here British Boy?"

"I'm here," a deep, gorgeous voice sounded with its familiar English accent.

I shut the door again and lifted part of the scarf over my head. I didn't know why it mattered if he knew who I was, but for some reason, I loved the idea of having anonymity for once. Scarf in place, I stepped into the dark room and shuffled along the tiled floor to the same spot I'd sat last week.

"Did you just walk in here with a scarf on your head?" British Boy asked with amusement in his voice.

"Well yeah, we're still keeping our identities a secret, aren't we?" And it was a good thing I had worn the scarf because if he knew about it he was obviously looking at me.

He laughed. "That's one way to do it. Maybe I should find a paper bag to use in case I get here second next time."

Next time? A warm feeling filled my chest. I liked the idea that there would be a next time. Which was weird. I didn't know this guy. I didn't even know what he looked like. The only British guy I'd seen recently was at the football game on Friday...but he was a middle-aged man who had sat with a boy who looked like he was in middle school.

British Boy didn't sound like that boy had looked, but I had to ask. "You don't happen to be in middle school, are you?"

"Do I sound that young?" he asked.

I shrugged, though he couldn't see it. "Just wanted to make sure. It's a good idea to nail down a few particulars."

"I'm not in middle school. I go here."

I sighed, relieved. "Do you have a brother, by chance?"

He was quiet for a moment before he answered slowly, "Yeees? Why do you ask?"

"Just wondering." Okay, good. This guy was probably the older brother of the one I'd seen at the football game. Maybe he and his dad were at the game cheering on British Boy.

I wanted to ask him if he played football but resisted the urge because he'd probably feel his identity was being threatened. Plus, if I asked him that, then I'd have to answer more narrowed-down questions of his. And there were only twenty of us on the drill team, so it wouldn't be that hard to figure out who I was. And that would totally ruin the fun of these secret meetings.

But I still needed to be smart about this, because he could be a serial killer with a knife in his hand and I wouldn't even know it. Which reminded me of what Eliana had said. "You're not Janitor Earl, are you?"

He laughed, a deep chuckle that rumbled up from his chest. "Do I sound like our dashing janitor?"

I smiled. Dashing and Janitor Earl didn't belong in the same sentence. But the way British Boy said his name almost made it sound exotic. "You never know who's going to be hiding in a dark room these days." I unzipped my lunch box and pulled out the turkey sandwich I'd made. Having to eat breakfast at six in the morning made it impossible to skip lunch.

After taking a bite, I cleared my throat and said, "I know we're not supposed to tell each other who we are exactly, but I was wondering if we could give each other more info. I mean, it's cool that I know you're from England, but I want to make sure I'm not talking to some little freshman boy...not that it would be bad if you're a freshman. I can still talk to you if you are."

Why did I say that? But I knew why. I was intrigued by him and it wasn't just because he was nice. His voice sounded hot and so I figured *he* might be hot, too. But I couldn't see myself thinking about a freshman boy that way. I may only be a junior, but I still didn't want to date anyone much younger than me.

Wait. I wasn't interested in dating anyone at all. Wasn't I supposed to be taking some time for myself? That's what I told that freshman boy last week anyway.

Okay, slow down, Ashlyn. You don't even know this guy. You need to be smarter this time.

"What grade are you anyway?" I asked as nonchalantly as I could.

"I'm a senior."

Senior.

Nice.

Not that I cared.

"What about you?" he asked.

"Junior." I shifted against the cupboards, trying to get more comfortable.

"Now that we've gotten that out of the way, how about we learn a few other things," he suggested with a smile in his voice. "I'd love to know more about you."

6

LUKE

OK, Luke. It's time to set your genius plan into motion. Operation "Get Back at Ashlyn" was ready to go. I'd have to ease her into it, of course—ask the easy questions before nailing down the juicy ones. But before I realized what I was saying, I asked, "What's your most embarrassing moment?" *Great job, Luke. That's not suspicious or anything.*

She was quiet for a moment, and I figured she might have realized something was up. Definitely should've eased my way into that question.

"My most embarrassing moment?" She said the words slowly. "If I tell you that, it would probably give away my identity."

Dang it. Wrong question. I should've guessed those "boyfriend wanted" posters would be high up on her list.

Well, if nothing else, I guess I could be proud I had succeeded in creating the most embarrassing moment for Ashlyn Brooks.

I cleared my throat. "Okay, so if you don't want to tell me your most embarrassing moment, what about telling me your biggest fear?" If she was afraid of mice or snakes, I could use that to my advantage.

"You want my real answer, or the one I tell everyone?" she asked.

"The real one, of course. That's the whole point of meeting in the dark, right?"

She was quiet again as she messed around with something in her lunchbox—which wasn't full of tarantulas after all. I wished I'd been smart enough to bring something to eat. She crumpled something like a plastic wrapper and said, "I guess I have to say that my biggest fear is that I'll never be good enough for the people in my life."

I hadn't expected that. It took me a moment before I could speak. "What makes you say that?"

"My mom, for example, is always trying to keep me on a super strict diet because she's worried I'll gain weight like she did at my age. And if it's not my diet, it's how well I'm doing in school. Or she worries she should get me a tutor because I got a C in Biology last year. It just feels like I'm never good enough for her. And then there's this guy I dated last year who made me feel like I could never do anything right. He was always getting after me about something, or worried that I was cheating on him just because I talked to a guy in class. It was like he was looking for the perfect, obedient girlfriend, and I just never matched up no matter how hard I tried. And believe me, I tried. I practically made myself crazy trying to keep him from getting angry."

Wow, I had no idea. Not only was her mom super controlling, but Noah had been crazy possessive. I always knew there was something up with him, but I didn't know this was what was going on with them last year. My heart went out to her with those words. And they also made me mad. I wasn't supposed to feel sorry for Ashlyn. She humiliated me in the absolute worst way at the football game. She wasn't supposed to make me feel a warmth of compassion in my chest.

But maybe I could work with this secret of hers. I wasn't just trying to find juicy details about her, I was also trying to make her fall in love with a fake guy.

"You shouldn't have to feel like you need to be good enough for someone," I said. "Anyone who treats you like garbage doesn't deserve to have you in their life."

"Are you a real guy?" she asked, amusement in her tone. "Because I've never met anyone as deep and understanding as you."

I smiled. This was so going to work. "Yeah. This is me. In the flesh. Maybe it's just my London breeding, and the fact that my mom raised me jolly good."

"Jolly good?" She laughed. "Do you guys actually say *jolly good* over there still? I thought it was just something from old movies."

I had no clue what I was doing. "Yeah, uh, me and my buddies used to joke around, saying old phrases like that while we had our afternoon tea and crumpets."

"That's still a tradition? What are crumpets anyway?" Ashlyn asked. "I've never had them."

Why was I saying all these things? I was in way over my head. "A crumpet is like a cracker?" My voice went up at the end, giving away how unsure I was about my answer. I really needed to study up on my English culture if I wanted to have a chance at pulling off the biggest prank of all time.

"Are they any good?" she asked.

"They're delicious." *I think. Change the subject, Luke!* My leg bounced up and down as I tried to figure out something to say. What had we been talking about before the crumpets? Oh, yeah. Noah. "So this boyfriend of yours, does he go to school here?"

"Yep. But thankfully, he's graduating this year. He's been a pain ever since we broke up. He's actually the reason why I was crying the last time we met."

She hadn't been crying because of me?

"It's my experience that if the guy is still giving you a hard time after you've broken up, he probably misses you." I put as much British passion in my voice as I could to make it come across even sweeter.

"Thanks for saying that. I want to believe you but—I don't know, I guess part of me has a hard time not believing that what he said was true. Like, maybe I really was a waste of time."

Noah told Ashlyn she was a waste of time? I might not be the nicest guy, but I would never say that to a girl I dated. Sure things didn't always end well, that was high school. We weren't meant to be forever. But I'd never call one of my girlfriends a waste of time.

"I'll just say this, I've only spent a short amount of time with you, and none of those moments seemed like a waste. In fact, they're probably the best moments I've had in a long time." I clapped my mouth shut after admitting those words, because they were true. Even though they shouldn't have been after everything we'd done to each other. Ashlyn might be hard to deal with sometimes, but there was something about her I couldn't get enough of. She was sweet and fun, and she had helped me out a ton last year even if she didn't know it.

When my mom was in the final stages of cancer, I had needed something to keep my mind off the future I knew was coming. It was gut-wrenching watching my mom die slowly before my eyes. So I'd come up with a plan to mess around with Ashlyn during Foods class. And even though it had probably been annoying to her to have her recipes screwed up, she'd played along and helped keep me sane. It wasn't the healthiest way to deal with my life, but it was therapeutic in its own twisted way. Which was why I had started our prank war again on the first day of school.

But maybe I'd gone too far, especially now that I was hearing how bad the people in her life had made her feel because of it. I may not have been the reason why she was crying last week, but I was responsible for it in a way. Noah wouldn't have had a reason to say whatever he said to her if I hadn't posted those stupid flyers everywhere.

"So now that you know my biggest fear," Ashlyn said, breaking me away from my thoughts. "What's yours?"

"My biggest fear already came true."

Why did I say that? I wasn't supposed to be opening up to her for real.

"It did? Was your biggest fear about moving here?"

Sure. I'd go with that. I didn't feel like talking about my mom today anyway. "Yep. Moving away from good old England was my biggest fear."

"Have you been able to make many friends yet?" she asked.

"Yeah, I have a bunch of friends." Did she think my British persona was a loner?

"Good." Her tone sounded relieved. "I just wanted to make sure everyone here in Ridgewater was treating you well."

"I'm getting along fine now." Yeah, she thought I was a loser who didn't know how to make friends. I guess it made sense, since she found me hiding here on the first day of school.

"That's a relief. Being new to a country must be hard, so I totally understand if you spend a lot of time in here alone. But just in case you ever wonder, I'm here to tell you that the people of Ridgewater welcome you."

I chuckled, somewhat touched that she cared that much about a guy she didn't really know. "Thank you for telling me that, Mystery Girl."

"You're welcome. I hadn't heard your voice around school yet, and no one else seemed to know about a new British boy...so I just wanted to make sure that you're doing okay."

"You were asking around about me?" That couldn't be good. It wouldn't take her long to figure out that my accent was fake.

"Don't sound so smug. I was worried about you." She sounded embarrassed, as if caught at being curious about me. Could it be possible that she was already interested in British Boy? This plan was going even better than I thought.

"I'm doing okay. I have a lot of friends. I was only hiding that day because the school counselor had her minions coming to befriend me." Befriend me, console me. They were close enough.

"Why?"

I definitely couldn't answer that question. I didn't think Ashlyn knew about my mom dying, since I hadn't told anyone besides Kellen and Jake. But if she did hear about it somehow, there was a chance that she'd connect the dots if British Boy's mom had died this summer as well. So I'd have to lie.

"The school counselor was worried about me fitting in, but like I said, I'm fine." Part of me wished I could tell her the truth. Kellen and Jake had gotten super awkward when I told them about my mom, but there was something about Ashlyn and these secret conversations of ours that made me think I might be able to open up to her.

Too bad I'd started this strange friendship on a foundation of lies.

"Our school counselor can be pretty pushy sometimes."

Ashlyn had to meet with our school counselor too? She didn't seem the type. "You have much experience with her?"

"Oh, um," she said nervously. "My grades started slipping last year when I was dating my ex. She just wanted to make sure everything was okay."

That didn't seem right. Was she not telling me everything about her and Noah's relationship? I wanted to ask more but figured I should wait for another time. I didn't want to spook her after our second meeting. If I wanted this prank to work, I needed to take my time.

So I readied to stand and said, "That's all I have time for today. I wasn't smart enough to bring my own lunch."

Her lunchbox scraped against the floor as it slid across to me. "You can have the rest of mine if you want," she said. "I made enough for two."

She made enough for both of us? Her thoughtfulness caught me off guard. I'd never met a high school girl who would do something like that.

"That's so thoughtful of you. Really, really thoughtful. But I need to meet up with my friends for lunch. Because I have friends, you know." I couldn't keep the smile out of my voice when I remembered how she assumed I didn't have any friends. How lame did she think I was?

I pushed the lunchbox back to her.

She cleared her throat. "Thanks for meeting me again. You're so easy to talk to, and honestly, I haven't even told my best friends about No— I mean about my ex-boyfriend and his temper."

I gritted my teeth at the thought of Noah treating her so terribly. I probably wouldn't hold off tackling him today at football practice. He deserved to be crushed by someone.

"Do you want me to go out first?" Ashlyn asked. "Since I was smart and brought my trusty scarf, that is." There was a cute laugh in her voice, and I couldn't keep from smiling at it.

"That would probably be a good idea. I'll make sure to bring my super cool Batman mask next time or something."

She giggled again. "You have a Batman mask? Batman is my favorite superhero."

"You like superheroes?" I asked. "Does that mean you prefer superhero movies over cheesy chick flicks?"

"Cheesy romance movies are kind of my thing. But I do

watch a good superhero movie now and then. I mean, me and my best friend do let my brother have a say sometimes."

"It was nice talking to you again, Mystery Girl."

"You too, British Boy." She paused for a moment, hesitating. "Do you want to try to meet again sometime? If we don't set up something now, we won't know when to meet."

"How about Thursday?" The words were out before I had a chance to stop myself.

"Thursday is perfect. I will *not* see you then." And with that she went out the door and into the light, and I was left feeling as confused as ever.

7

ASHLYN

THE NEXT TWO days dragged on as I anxiously awaited my next secret meeting with British Boy. Our last conversation had been so good—I'd never been able to talk to anyone like that before. He was deep and understanding, and I didn't know how he did it but he knew just the right things to say to me. It was like he was the perfect British gentleman that I'd dreamed up from years of watching my favorite BBC movies, and he had magically come to sweep me off my feet when I needed him most. I would be absolutely crazy not to jump at the chance to meet with him again.

I tried to do my best to keep with our agreement of not trying to figure out who he really was, but it was so hard not to perk my ears up everywhere I went, with the off chance that I might get to hear his silky-smooth, delicious voice again.

"Great practice today, girls," Coach Meyer said after we'd finished going through our military routine during Thursday morning practice. I still didn't know how she could be so happy and energetic at this time of day. But I guessed that's what happens when you get paid to do something you're passionate about. And boy was she passionate about dance. I almost thought she'd become a Math teacher just so she could be the drill coach as well.

She waved for us to gather around her. "I have one item of business to go over before you ladies head to first period."

I took a sip from my water bottle and sat on the dance lab's wooden floor to give my legs a rest after our hour-and-a-half practice.

"Principal Baker approached me yesterday about an opportunity for some of you girls. One of our students here at Ridgewater High was diagnosed with leukemia and the faculty thought it would be great if our school did a fundraiser to help pay for the treatments."

"Who is it?" our drill captain, also known as a professional busy-body, Kelsie Perkins interrupted.

"Lacey Sparling," Coach answered. "She's a freshman this year."

Kelsie made a show of frowning, which looked totally fake. "Aww, that is so sad."

"Yes, it's very sad." Coach nodded. "Anyway, Principal Baker suggested we could do our own version of *Dancing with the Stars* since Lacey is a dancer as well and loves that show. He also wanted to know if you girls would be willing to choreograph a dance and teach it to one of the stars of our school."

"Stars of the school?" Kelsie interrupted again. "Like the drill team captain, perhaps?"

I rolled my eyes. Kelsie was insufferable.

Coach gave Kelsie an annoyed look. "Possibly, though you'll have to talk to the principal and student body president to find out who exactly they have in mind."

"They better not just pick guys, because that would be so unfair," Madison, Kelsie's sidekick, said.

"I have no idea what they're planning." Coach looked sternly at Madison. "I was just asked to find a few girls to help. If you're worried about it, you can talk to the people in charge and offer suggestions. But if they happen to only pick guys since it's hard to find male partners who can teach a girl to dance, go ahead and think of yourself as the stars of the night. You'll be dancing and showing off your choreography in front of a lot of people, so you'll be in the spotlight just as much as the dancers they ask. This is not about who is more popular, it's about raising money to help Lacey."

I checked the time on my phone. The bell was about to ring, and I still had to change out of my dance clothes and fix my hair. I would be meeting British Boy during lunch after all—not that it mattered what I looked like. He shouldn't be seeing my face anyway.

I raised my hand in the air. "Do we have to choreograph ballroom-type dances, like they do on the real show?" I may have danced for most of my life, but that didn't mean I knew the difference between the tango and the rumba.

"I don't think it matters. They just want a dance that's entertaining and well done."

"Then I can help," I said. My mom was always helping with different charities, maybe she'd think I was doing something with my life if I started following in her footsteps.

Coach Meyer brightened at my offer. "Thank you, Ashlyn. I appreciate it." She tapped on her tablet for a moment, probably typing in my name, and then looked up at the rest of the team expectantly. "You can go ahead and change, Ashlyn. Someone will let you know the details when we have them."

I stood, relieved I'd have time to get ready after all. When I walked past Kelsie and Madison, I couldn't help but notice their sour expressions. I just smiled back.

AS SOON AS the lunch bell rang, I rushed down the halls to get to the Chemistry lab. I'd made sure to make myself lunch again, and had taken it with me to class so I wouldn't have to stop by my locker before heading to meet British Boy. I didn't want to miss a moment of our time together just because my stomach was hungry. Every minute was invaluable, and I couldn't have Luke or anyone else making me late again.

I got stuck in a traffic jam in the A hall but found one of the tall football players pushing himself through the crowd, so I followed right behind him.

I drew in a deep breath once I made it to the lab.

"Is anyone in here?" I asked, like I had on Monday.

"Yes, and you're late again."

I smiled. That voice! He could read the dictionary to me and I would hang onto every single word. I put my scarf over my head and snuck in.

"Sorry I got stuck in the hall. I really was hurrying." I shut the door, letting the darkness envelop me in its mystery.

He laughed. "It's okay. You gave me plenty of time to find a more comfortable spot to sit."

"Where are you?" I could tell his voice was coming from farther away than it had been last time.

"I'm in the back corner."

"Do you mind if I join you?"

"Not at all. Come on over. I even brought a blanket, so you wouldn't have to sit on the cold floor this time."

My heart swelled. He brought a blanket? He was so thoughtful!

I inched forward carefully, holding my hands out in front of me so I wouldn't accidentally bump into anything.

"I'm this way," he said, probably noticing my footsteps had veered in the wrong direction.

I righted my course and continued slowly. My hand brushed

against one of the lab tables. I used it as my guide until it ended. "This would be a lot easier if we could just turn on the lights, you know."

I heard his deep chuckle. "It would also ruin the fun."

I grinned, following his voice again. "True."

"Watch out for my feet," he said suddenly. "We don't want a repeat of our first meeting."

I stopped and felt around with the toe of my sandal, which hit what was probably the bottom of his shoe. "Which side should I sit on?"

"This side." I heard a soft patting sound. Probably his hand on the blanket.

I took the last couple of steps forward, without tripping over his feet I might add, and then slowly lowered myself down beside him. I misjudged the distance and ended up bumping against his shoulder. The skin on my arm immediately burst to life at the touch. I scooted an inch or so from him, not wanting to scare him away or anything.

But I had touched British Boy! He was real!

"So what do you want to talk about today?" I asked, feeling all jittery with nerves.

"I'm not sure. Last time we got really deep. Do you want to keep it light and just get to know each other better?"

"But I thought we were supposed to be scuba diving. Don't you have to go down deep to do that?" I asked with a smile on my lips. My cheeks were going to be so sore today. Being around him just made me happy for some reason. Like a kid in Disneyland.

"Okay, whatever you want. I'm just happy to be with you again. I don't care what we talk about."

Was it possible he was as intrigued by me as I was with him? Someone needed to pinch me so I would know this wasn't some sort of dream. Guys didn't ever want to just be with me.

I drew in a breath, hoping it would help calm my mind which

was running away with thoughts of how too good to be true this guy seemed to be.

"Ask me the first question that pops into your head," I said.

"Really?" He sounded unsure.

"Yes. I'm an open book in here."

"What was the happiest moment in your life?"

Right now!

But I couldn't say that because he might think I was crazy. We were supposed to be honest...but not *that* honest.

"Hmm..." I thought about it.

"You're not about to tell me that it was when you looked up at the sky this morning and saw it was blue again, are you?"

I laughed. He was too perfect! "No. I was actually thinking about the question."

"Just checking."

"I don't know if I could choose just one, but if I have to, I'd say that my happiest moment was just playing in the ocean this summer when my family rented a house in the Hamptons for a couple of weeks."

"Really?"

"Yeah, after everything with No— I mean, with my ex-boyfriend, it was nice to just relax and have fun again. My best friend came with us, and we had the funnest time letting the ocean push and pull us along the shore."

"That does sound nice. I wish I'd had your summer." There was a somber tone to his voice, and I remembered what he'd said on Monday about moving here being his biggest fear.

"You must miss your friends back home."

"What?" He paused, and then cleared his throat. "I mean, yeah. I do. They were great. We didn't do cool things like play in the ocean though."

"That's right. You had your daily tea and crumpets. I wonder if I could buy any here somewhere?"

"I don't think you can. I actually looked for them when I went to the store yesterday."

"You said they're crackers, right?"

"Did I say cracker? I actually meant a griddle cake."

"What's a griddle cake?" I'd never heard of those before

"Kind of like the English muffins you have here."

"But they're not the same thing."

"No. According to an article I read...one time...for a report I did in school, crumpets are made with butter while English muffins aren't. And a crumpet is made from a batter and cooked only on one side, but an English muffin is made from dough and toasted on both sides."

"Wow, you really did your research. I'm surprised you remembered those small details."

"I had a lot of time on my hands." He shifted to get more comfortable. "Anyway, enough about that boring stuff. Let's get back to our scuba diving. I want to know everything there is to know about you, Mystery Girl."

I smiled, loving how his interest and sincerity made me feel. "Then ask me another question. I'll tell you anything you want to know."

"Anything? Hmm..." He grew quiet, thinking. "Do you make your bed in the morning?"

I laughed. I didn't expect that one. "So we're going with surface level now?"

"It's a very telling question. You can learn a lot about a person based on whether they make their bed or not." There was a hint of a smile in his voice that I loved.

"Okay, fine. Yes, I make my bed in the morning. I hate messes."

"Me too." Of course he did.

"My turn now. What's your favorite color?"

"Blue. And yours."

"Pink."

"Look how stereotypical we are. Okay, now for a harder one." His voice became suddenly more serious. "Do you think that life is fair?"

I pursed my lips. "What do you mean by that?"

He sighed, and I heard his head lean against the wall behind us. "Like, do you think that good people have mostly good things happen to them? And bad people have bad things happen to them?"

I thought about it for a minute. "I don't know. I don't think it's fair, exactly. But I think that a lot of times we can choose whether or not to do things based on what the consequence will be. I think hard work plays a much bigger role in whether things are *fair* for us."

"Like a 'you make your own luck' kind of thing?"

"Yes. Exactly."

"Okay, but what if you were to, say, write the best song in the whole universe, but only one person hears it so it never makes you any money. But then a really famous singer puts a few catchy lyrics on repeat to an upbeat sound and it immediately races high in rankings just because he's well known. Did their hard work pay off? Is that fair?"

"Maybe the first person should have worked harder to get their song heard."

"Okay, fine. Bad scenario." He exhaled. "What about this—say there's a person who did everything in their power to live a healthy life. They never ate junk food. Ate veggies like they were going out of style. Exercised regularly. Got enough sleep. And then they go to the doctor one day and find out they have a terminal illness. Did their hard work pay off?"

I shrugged, not having an answer. I thought about the girl we were doing a fundraiser for, and how she was only fourteen and fighting for her life. "Are you talking about Lacey? Did you hear about her, too?"

"Lacey?" He was quiet for a moment. "No. I don't know a Lacey. Someone else I was close to had...Parkinson's Disease."

"How close?" From the somber tone of his voice, it sounded like they were pretty close.

"My, um, my grandma had it before she died."

"And you were close to your grandma?"

He sighed. "She practically raised me."

"Oh, I'm so sorry," I said, not knowing what else to say.

Should I scoot closer and hug him? He spoke before I had time to decide.

"It's okay. It happened a long time ago."

"It can still be hard though."

He sighed again. "Yes, it can."

We were quiet for a while, and I tried to figure out this boy. He was so different from other guys I knew at school. He was deep and emotional. And I was having a hard time believing that he was actually real. Maybe it was the magic of the dark room, but I never knew it was possible to get this close to someone in just a few conversations.

"How about another question," I suggested eventually.

"Another question would be great."

"If you had to choose just one food to eat for the rest of your life, what would you pick?"

"Easy! Pizza. You can vary the toppings and make it anything. What about you?"

"I could say the same thing about salad, and make my mom so proud. But I think I'm gonna have to agree with you. I'd definitely pick pizza."

We got lost in conversation after that. It was amazing how easy he was to talk to. The conversation just flowed, with no awkward pauses. It was like we had known each other forever, not just a week. And when the warning bell rang, I realized that I'd completely forgotten to eat my lunch. I hadn't even thought about it once.

"Should we do this again sometime?" I stood, lifting my full lunchbox from the floor.

"Are you busy on Tuesday during lunch?" he asked, and I was so relieved he hadn't grown bored of me yet.

"Tuesday is perfect." And then I left, knowing these lunch periods were moving higher and higher on my happiest moments list.

8

LUKE

MY STOMACH WAS GRUMBLING by the time Ashlyn and I finished our conversation. These secret meetings were getting a lot deeper than I'd expected, and I was revealing way more about myself than I'd planned. I was starting to wonder if the whole prank idea was actually worth continuing. *What if I slip up?* Like messing up by calling crumpets crackers last week. Sure, I'd corrected my mistake today, and I didn't think she had realized what I'd done, but that was a very lucky break. And then I almost ruined things again when I brought up the whole fairness-in-terminal-illness thing. But she seemed to buy the grandma story so that should be okay too. Most everyone I knew had someone in their life who had died from a terminal illness, which was sad that it was true, but maybe if I didn't run off on any more tangents in the future I could keep this whole charade up.

And I really wanted to keep this thing going, even if I never used any of this for some huge prank of all pranks. Because already the thought of not having someone to open up to was suffocating. And it seemed like she enjoyed our time together just as much as I did. I'd worried she might not like the blanket-on-the-floor gesture, but she totally loved it. And sitting next to her had been nice. She smelled amazing, and the sensations from when she accidentally bumped against my arm hadn't been half bad either.

I'd purposely not worn any cologne today, since I didn't want to give her any clues about who I really was, but maybe I could find a new scent just for British Boy to wear during our lunch meetings.

As soon as she was out of the Chemistry lab, I folded up the blanket and stuffed it in my backpack. I'd have to bring it next time too. Maybe I'd even bring something else to sweeten the deal. Chocolates, possibly? I'd have to add "ways to win over a girl" into my research for tonight. Not that *I* was trying to win over Ashlyn. I'd only need that stuff in case British Boy decided he wanted to finish off the prank. Until then, I would just see where this new friendship took us.

MAX KNOWLES, the student body president, stopped me on my way to football practice.

"Hey, Luke." Max pushed his hipster glasses up farther on his nose. "I need to ask you a question."

"I have to get to practice, so make it quick."

He bit his lip, as if thinking over the next words. I wasn't going to like whatever he had to say. "I don't know if you heard about this yet, but one of the kids in school was just diagnosed with leukemia. And the faculty and student government came up with a plan to help her and her family out. They don't have good enough insurance to cover all the treatments, so we thought we'd hold a fundraising event for her."

This must be the girl Ashlyn had mentioned earlier. The girl with cancer. Oh how I hated cancer. And Max probably knew that. Which meant he knew what my answer already was.

I crossed my arms. "What's this fundraising event going to be and what do I have to do?"

Max looked down at his shoes for a second before meeting my eyes. "They thought it would be fun to have a Dancing with the Stars of Ridgewater High night. Kind of like the show but with the stars of our school. And since you're the football captain, we wanted to ask you to help us out."

"Dancing?" I was about the worst dancer I knew of.

"Yes, dancing. We have a few volunteers from the drill team willing to teach you guys."

"The drill team, you say?" I asked, my interest sparked.

"Yeah, so far we have Kelsie Perkins, Avery Sinter, Camilla Reyes, Ashlyn Brooks, Trinity Weaver..."

Ashlyn.

After Max had finished saying a few more names that I didn't recognize, he asked, "So, what will it be? You willing to help Lacey out?"

I drew in a deep breath, trying to talk myself out of what I was going to say. Dancing in front of the school was about the last thing I wanted to do. But cancer? I hated cancer and I hated the idea of a family not only worried about fighting the horrible disease, but also possibly being financially ruined because of it. We'd been lucky enough with my mom to have awesome insurance. I couldn't imagine having to worry about more than just getting her better.

I pinched my eyes shut for second and said, "Okay, I'll do it."

Max's face brightened like I just saved the world or something. "Thank you, Luke. We really appreciate it."

9

ASHLYN

"YOU PARTNERED ME WITH WHO?" I couldn't believe my ears. There was no way in the world they would put me and Luke together for this dancing competition. Didn't they pay attention to anything that went on at our school?

"We asked Luke who he thought would make the best coach and partner for him. He looked over the list and immediately said your name." Max Knowles looked as shocked as I felt. "I wasn't about to argue with him. Getting guys to do this thing was hard enough."

"But I have to dance with Luke?" We could barely stand each other. And he wanted to spend hours upon hours alone with me?

Max looked around the hall before saying in a low voice, "Think of it this way, you're in charge during your practice sessions. You get to choose the choreography. You can decide how to spend your time together. You can make it as painful as you like. But in all honesty, I hope you'll work well together. This event means so much to a lot of people at our school. We want it to be the best it can be."

I shook my head, still baffled at the prospect of teaching Luke

Davenport a dance. I'd just have to come up with something that didn't involve a lot of physical contact. Although, I had to admit that his arms would probably feel nice. Those muscles. I shook my head again. Those muscles were attached to Luke. And Luke was... I thought back to our last interaction. Luke had been nice. He said he wanted to mend things between us. Maybe he was being honest. I'd just have to wait and see. Who knew, maybe he was turning over a new leaf, and maybe this partnership of ours could finally get us out of our war once and for all. I smiled at the thought. And if it didn't, I could torture him by making him wear tights.

MONDAY AT LUNCH, Max called a meeting for all the dance contestants to figure out the details of the event. There were only eleven guys who'd agreed to do it, Luke being one of them. To my dismay, Noah was there as well. I was suddenly thankful Luke had chosen to be my partner, so I wouldn't have to dance with Noah.

"Thank you all for coming here. I'm hoping we can make this quick as I know you're anxious to get your lunch." Max looked around at the group of drill team members with their partners. I'd never guessed they'd have jocks competing against chess club members and band nerds, but Max had done a great job of finding guys from almost every group at school. And from the way most of them were standing, the guys all seemed pretty uncomfortable to be here, regardless of their popularity status.

Max continued, "Each of you has been paired up with a partner. You have one chance to wow the crowd and the judges with your choreographed dance. When the night is over, the judges will announce the winners and the winners will have bragging rights for the rest of their life."

"Yeah, I'm totally putting this on my scholarship applications," Luke said so everyone could hear. A low rumble of laughter spread throughout the room. I couldn't help but smile too, because even though Luke did cause a lot of drama in my life he could always make me laugh.

"Each partnership will pick a number from this," Max said, holding up a clear bowl containing a bunch of folded white papers. "And it'll decide the order of the performance."

We all got in line to pick our fate. I somehow ended up sandwiched between Luke and Noah. As we waited for the line to move forward, Noah leaned next to my ear and said in a low voice, "Too bad we aren't partners. I was hoping to spend a little more time with you, since you're so desperate to get a boyfriend again."

"But wasn't I just a waste of time?" I shrugged him off my shoulder and looked him straight in the eyes. "I'd never dance with you, Noah. Not even if you were the last guy at school. I'd rather dance with my dog."

"You pretty much are." Noah eyed Luke whose posture stiffened at Noah's comment.

"Luke isn't a dog. Let's just hope you and Madison can work together, because once you see Luke and me on the dance floor, you'll want to run in the opposite direction."

Luke turned back to face me at the mention of us winning. "I wouldn't be bragging about our dancing skills just yet. I can't dance to save my life."

"Then why did you agree to do this in the first place?" I asked.

He looked down and shoved his hands in his pockets. "I have my reasons."

We made it to the front of the line. Luke reached into the bowl and pulled out a slip of paper. His brow furrowed when he saw our number. "We're eleventh?"

My stomach shriveled at his words. "That means we're last.

Which means, we have to be a showstopper."

"I'll just grab a different one real quick," Luke said. But Noah had heard us and shoved his hand in the bowl to grab the last paper.

"You got it. You're dancing it," Noah said with a competitive glint in his eyes. I wanted to smack him.

Max cleared his throat to get our attention again. "Now that you've chosen your numbers, please tell me what they are so I can write them down. Then make sure to arrange a time to practice with your partners. I know quite a few of you are busy with your sports and other activities, so I really do appreciate you taking the time to do this. If you have any more questions, you can ask me or Coach Meyer. The event is on October twenty-first, which only gives you about a month and a half, so make sure you don't waste any time."

Then he left us to figure everything out on our own.

I glanced at Luke, who was still staring at the paper in his hands.

"I have drill practice every morning before school, and then again on Thursday evenings and some Saturdays, so that's probably going to be a little tricky to get together," I said. "And I know you have football after school and games every Friday, so maybe the best time for us to get together would be later in the evenings on weekdays. Or possibly on the weekends?"

Luke nodded. "Evenings are good. There's not much going on at home these days, so that should be wide open."

The way he said that made me wonder if something had changed recently in his home life. And there was a sadness in his eyes that hadn't been there a moment before. I'd have to learn more about Luke when we get together next time.

We arranged to meet at his house that night at seven to find out what I had to work with. I just hoped we'd be able to get along well enough to make this new partnership work.

10

LUKE

ASHLYN KNOCKED on my door exactly at seven, wearing what I guessed were her dancing workout clothes: a loose pink t-shirt and tight black pants. I tried not to look too long at her because even in her workout clothes she was hot. And I really shouldn't be thinking that right now.

"Thanks for agreeing to meet here." I led her into the living room that used to seem so warm and inviting when Mom was alive. Now it just felt lonely. Like the life had disappeared from the house the same moment she slipped away.

Ashlyn smiled as she looked around the living room, glancing at the photos on the walls of my brother, my parents, and me. She stopped in front of the family picture we had taken last spring with my mom in her wig.

"So this is the famous Davenport family." Her eyes sparkled.

I dropped my gaze, shuffling my weight between my feet. I didn't want to answer any questions about my family. Tonight was supposed to be about dancing.

Did I just think that tonight was about dancing? What world was I living in?

She moved, so I looked up. Now she was inspecting my photo, and then the one of my mom and dad.

"You and your mom look a lot alike. She's beautiful."

"Does that mean you think I'm beautiful?" I asked, hoping to steer the conversation away from my mom. Ashlyn still didn't seem to know about my mom's passing. Looks like the school counselor hadn't told everyone yet. Which was probably good.

Ashlyn laughed, and her eyes crinkled at the corners when she did. "I said your *mom* is beautiful. But you do have her eyes."

I walked toward the couch and sat down. "How about we get started? I have a feeling we'll be spending a lot of time with each other over the next several weeks if we're going to pull together something decent."

"You're probably right." Ashlyn stuck her hands on her hips and seemed to give me a good look over. "To start, we'll need to figure out where you are with your dancing ability. I mean, the school did get a good preview of your potty-dance style moves at the game two Fridays ago, but I'm not sure that's what Max is hoping for in our show."

I scowled. "You just had to go there, didn't you?"

"I'll go there as often as I can." Ashlyn beamed. "You deserve it."

"I don't know if anyone deserves to have Icy Hot *down there*. No matter how badly they may have humiliated you with certain posters on the first day of school. Plus, didn't you get like a ton of guys' numbers from that? You should be thanking me."

"Yeah, I got a bunch of your friends' numbers, and I don't think they were really interested. They didn't even try to follow up the next day."

"Well, Jake and Kellen aren't known for their long attention spans when it comes to girls. You should know their type, though. Isn't your brother of the same mold?"

"Must be a high-school-boy thing," she said.

I shook my head. "Not for me."

"Not for you? Really?" Her voice dripped with so much disbelief that it made me wonder what kinds of lies my ex-girlfriends may have spread about me. "How is your dating record so much better? You haven't had a girlfriend in the time I've known you."

I'd been too worried about my mom to think about dating anyone last spring. But now that she was gone, I had to admit that it might be nice to have someone who cared about me.

I shrugged. "Maybe my record isn't necessarily better, just different. When I ask a girl to be my girlfriend, she can count on me sticking with it for a while. I'm not a flavor-of-the-week kind of guy." *Why was I saying this?* Probably because she told me about Noah in the Chemistry lab, and for some reason, I wanted her to know that not all guys were jerks when it came to dating.

"Let's see if you're as good at learning as you are at bragging." Ashlyn stepped forward and gestured for me to stand before her.

I stood about six inches taller than her, which was a good height difference, I guess. Though I had no idea if it was good for dancing. At least she didn't make me feel like a giant.

Ashlyn inspected me as I stood there. I stuffed my hands in my pockets to keep from fidgeting as she walked a circle around me, tapping her chin with her fingers. Once she was done, she said, "You already have good posture, so that's good. Most tall guys slouch, so that's something you have going for you. But when you dance, you need to be hyperaware of your lines. Just keep that in mind, okay?"

"Got it. Long, straight lines."

"Very good." She looked up at me with her bright blue eyes. "Do you have a speaker I can hook my phone up to?"

"Yeah." I took the phone she held out, our fingers brushing as I did so. I tried not to notice the shock of electricity that came from her touch. That wasn't supposed to happen with Ashlyn.

I crossed the room to the entertainment center and plugged

her phone into the speaker. When I turned around, I jumped back. She was right behind me.

"Sorry to startle you." Ashlyn stepped back as well. "I just wanted to turn on a song."

"You're not going to teach me anything first?"

She shook her head as she tapped on her phone. "I need to see what I have to work with."

Which meant she was planning to watch me dance. Any confidence I might have had drained from my blood.

An upbeat song played through the speakers.

"Let's see your moves." Ashlyn crossed her arms and waited for me to dance.

My feet were frozen to the floor, suddenly full of lead.

She arched her eyebrow. "We don't have all night, Luke. Just show them to me. I promise I won't laugh."

So she expected me to suck at this. I didn't know if that was a good thing or a bad thing, but at least her expectations were spot on.

"Here, just do what I do," she said. She started stepping from side to side to the beat, letting her head hang back with her eyes closed, her long blonde hair cascading behind her. She made it look so easy, dancing in front of me. I could never do that. I was way too self-conscious.

She opened her eyes a moment later and stopped dancing. "I'm not here for you to just watch. Move."

I released a heavy breath and stepped to the right. My left foot followed and then moved back to where it began. It was kind of like what Ashlyn had done, a sort of step-touch, step-touch move...albeit much stiffer than the way she'd done it.

"That's a start," she said. She stepped closer and set her hands on my shoulders. I shivered at her unexpected touch. "You need to loosen your shoulders up, get some arm movement going." She gave my shoulders a shake.

I swallowed and tried to catch the beat of the song before stepping to the side again. This time I snapped my fingers with each step.

"Are you dancing like Hitch?"

"Who's Hitch?"

She waved her hand. "It's an old movie my mom loves. Will Smith plays this guy named Hitch who is, like, the ultimate ladies' man, and he coaches other guys on how to land the girl of their dreams. That's exactly what he looks like when he's teaching Albert how to dance."

"So is that a good thing or not?"

She laughed. "It's fine. I'm pretty sure most of the *cool guys* dance like that."

Ok, as long as it was fine. Fine was better than terrible.

She kept stepping like that for a minute, and I was getting more confident in my dancing ability until she did some twirly-leap-thingy and turned back to me, expecting me to follow.

I just stood there, my mouth hanging open like a doofus. "Do I have to learn how to do that?"

She looked back at me and smiled. "No, sorry. I couldn't help myself. Sometimes the music just gets to me and I have to leap. Dancing like you is so boring."

"It may be boring, but at least I don't look like some pansy prancing around in tights."

She grinned, her eyes crinkling at the corners as she did. "I'm guessing you won't like the costume I had in mind for you, then."

I cocked my head to the side. "And that would be?" *Please don't say tights.*

"I was thinking of something like a Peter Pan costume. You look good in green, right?" Her face was so serious.

"Uh..."

She gently slapped my arm. "Totally joking. I haven't even had time to pick out a song, let alone a costume."

"Do I have a say in any of this?"

She tilted her head, her gaze looking me up and down. "That depends on how easy you are to work with."

I stood straighter and held my arm up as if giving my oath of honor in court. "I promise to be the perfect student."

She smiled. "Great. Have you ever done the waltz before?"

"The waltz?" I coughed. "Um, no. Pretty sure you've already witnessed the extent of my moves. Dancing isn't my thing."

"*Wasn't* your thing," she corrected. "I'm hoping for both of our sakes that it becomes your thing very soon."

She stepped closer until we were almost touching torsos, and she held my left hand in her right. She positioned my other hand to rest on her back, just below her shoulder blade. I sucked in a breath. Our sudden closeness took me off guard.

I wasn't supposed to react to Ashlyn like this. I was supposed to be pulling off the best prank ever by getting her to fall in love with a fake guy. She was already getting closer to figuring out that her British Boy wasn't real, and if I started acting nicer toward her, or get some *feelings* involved, the more likely she'd figure everything out.

It might be a good idea to purposely stomp on her toes to make sure she didn't realize I was softening.

Her left arm hugged around my tricep, her hand on my shoulder, and then she pulled in even closer. I sucked in another breath, which was bad because she smelled like coconut and something else—same as she smelled like in the Chemistry lab—and it was making me delirious.

She didn't seem to notice though, because she said, "For the waltz, we do a series of three steps to the beat. Begin by moving your left foot forward, just a small step."

I did as she said, and she mirrored me. That seemed simple enough.

"Now you need to step your right foot forward so it's in line with your other foot, about shoulder-width apart."

I did as she instructed, not even stepping on her foot. We were moving together.

So far, so good. I might have a chance.

"The next thing you need to do is to move your right foot so it's next to your left."

I tried to do as she said but ended up stepping on my own loose shoelace. So much for having a chance.

"Why are we doing the waltz anyway? Did you already make up our dance?"

"No, like I said, I haven't even picked a song. I just figured the waltz might be a simple way to start your feet moving in the right direction."

"And how are my feet doing?"

"They're okay. Just a bit stiff."

I stopped. It was hopeless. I might as well give up now. So much for helping out Lacey and her family.

She looked up at me, her eyes clouded with confusion. "Why'd you stop?"

"You said my dancing is stiff."

Her eyes softened. "Just relax, Luke. This is only the first practice. We still have over a month to nail this down. It'll be okay."

I ran a hand through my hair. "Fine."

She bit her glossy pink lip. "But we should probably practice again soon."

The dancing lesson went okay after that, but I definitely wouldn't be entering other dancing competitions anytime soon.

"When do you want to meet next?" she asked, once we were officially done.

I thought about it and had the idea to play with her a little bit.

"Um, since I'm guessing I'll need a lot of help, we could get together tomorrow at lunchtime. Wednesday is bad, I don't have time on Friday because of the game, and I'm sure you have better things to do this weekend than teach me how to dance. So, tomorrow would be the best time."

She bit her lip and her fingers twitched at her sides. "Tomorrow's Tuesday, right?" Tuesday was the day she was supposed to meet British Boy again.

"Do you have some sort of club meeting on Tuesdays?"

"No..." she said slowly, as if trying to come up with an excuse. "It's just that I have another one of those tutoring sessions with Mr. Phipps and I can't miss it."

She was lying through her teeth. But this was fun. "You really need that much help with History?"

"The genius gene skipped me at our house. Jess got the brains. Macey got the cuteness factor. And me...well, I'm just the dancer."

"You're also a great teacher," I offered, not liking the idea of her thinking so low about herself. She'd been awesome to help me out tonight. Not many girls at our school would have been so patient. "Needing help isn't something to be ashamed of. But if you really do have to go to this tutoring session, how about we get together for at least part of Saturday, if that's okay with you?"

"Saturday morning or afternoon?" she asked, pulling out her phone to check her schedule.

"Afternoon works. I gotta sleep in as much as I can. Growing boy and all."

She gave me what might have been interpreted as a flirtatious look. "Growing boy? More like growing man." She touched my bicep. "Dancing with a guy does have some perks, and I wouldn't call those guns of yours little at all."

My cheeks heated. *Ashlyn was flirting with me?* Had I heard her right?

"Thanks?" I cleared my throat after recovering from my

shock. Her cheeks were slightly pinker than usual. Had she not meant to say that out loud?

That thought sent an interesting sensation through my stomach.

She quickly grabbed her things, suddenly in a hurry to leave. "I'll, uh, see you on Saturday then. We can figure out the details of when and where later."

11

ASHLYN

"I TOLD Luke he has nice guns yesterday," I whispered to Eliana on Tuesday morning as we got our books out of our lockers. "I don't know what's happening to me."

Eliana smiled. "They do say that love and hate can be closely related. And he is hot."

"True. But I'm not supposed to flirt with him. I mean, I already have British Boy to keep my mind occupied. I don't have time to think about anyone else."

"How are things going with British Boy?" Eliana asked, her eyebrow raised. "Still planning to meet during lunch?"

I nodded. "That's the plan. Luke actually invited me to practice our dancing at that time. But I told him I have a tutoring session instead." I couldn't let him of all people find out that I sat in the dark during lunch talking to a guy who I'd never even seen before. He'd never let me live that down. Instead of putting "boyfriend wanted" posters all over the school, he'd change them to "invisible boyfriend wanted" posters and say I was desperate.

"I'm really curious about this boy. I keep eavesdropping on people in the hall just to see if I hear an English accent."

"I know. Me too. Sometimes I wish our school was smaller."

"Want me to hide somewhere close by and watch for him?" Eliana asked, a devious look on her face.

"I wish! But I promised him I wouldn't check around, so for now, no. But I might take you up on that later."

When I got to the Chemistry lab later that day, I opened the door and peeked in to check if British Boy was in there yet, but no one answered. So I slipped inside and waited for a few minutes. I was so nervous for some reason, having a hard time getting my breathing under control. Our last conversation had been really good, and I couldn't get him out of my mind.

I waited for what seemed like forever, but the door didn't open. When he still hadn't shown up a few more minutes later, I decided to get started on my lunch. When I'd finished my sandwich and had eaten about half of my carrot sticks, something slid through the gap under the door. I glanced at the time on my phone—about ten minutes left in the lunch period. Had British Boy just stood me up? That didn't seem like him. Hopefully he wasn't sick.

I packed my things back into my lunchbox and stood, using my flashlight app as a guide. There was a piece of paper on the floor by the door. I ran my hand along the wall until I found the light switch. The note was addressed to "Mystery Girl."

I quickly opened it and leaned against the cabinet behind me as I read the blocky handwriting.

Mystery Girl,

Sorry I couldn't show up today. Something came up and it looks like my lunch periods will be a lot busier from now on. Maybe we could email each other instead? If you're interested, just shoot an email to: britishboy@awesomemail.com. *I hope to hear from you. Please forgive me for standing you up. I really do think you're awesome.*

Sincerely,
British Boy

My heart sank. Our lunch meetings were over? Already? What could have come up?

I tried not to be too disappointed. At least he'd given me his email address. I smiled at the fact that he used the nickname that I'd given him as his email username. I quickly folded the note and slipped it into the back pocket of my jeans. After making sure the hall was clear, I stepped out into the light. When I turned around the corner, I ran right into Luke Davenport's chest.

He seemed surprised at our sudden meeting. "Oh hey, Ashlyn. How are you today?" He tipped his head down to look me over as if he thought something might be wrong.

"I'm doing great. My, um, tutoring session was good. Probably won't need them after today." I adjusted the strap of my bag on my shoulder.

Luke looked at me skeptically. "I didn't realize Mr. Phipp's classroom had moved to the same hall as the Chem lab."

My face heated. Had he just caught me in my lie? "My tutoring session ended a little while ago. I was just walking around the halls."

Luke nodded, not convinced. But I tried not to worry about whether he believed me or not. There was no way he could know about my meetings with British Boy, right?

But I should probably get away from him before he could ask any more questions. "Well, it was nice bumping into you. You still planning on Saturday?"

"Yep. I even watched a couple of episodes of that show after you left last night. So be prepared for me to really wow you with my excellent dancing skills."

I smiled at the thought of him taking things so seriously. There weren't many guys at school that I could imagine actually wanting to do well at this dancing thing. I figured most guys would just mess around and make a joke out of the whole thing. Madison had complained this morning about Noah doing just that during their practice. But Luke was surprising me all the time.

"BRITISH BOY and I are done with our secret meetings." I frowned when I met Eliana on our way to Spanish.

"Why?" she asked.

I hugged my books to my chest. "He didn't show up. And when I was leaving, I found this note that he'd slid under the door for me. He says he's busy during lunch now."

We turned the corner and squeezed through a tight area of the hall that was jam-packed with students. Once we had made it through, Eliana looked over her shoulder and said, "That stinks. But it'll be nice having you back at our table again. It was totally awkward being a third wheel to Jess and Stacy today."

"I can't believe they're still dating. It's already been like three weeks."

Eliana laughed. "I know. Maybe they're meant to be."

"Yeah, right."

"So, did British Boy leave you a way to contact him?" Eliana asked.

"He gave me his email address, so it's not like we're losing all contact. But I'm sad I won't get to hear his accent anymore."

"You'll just have to set Siri to speak like a British man. Then you can swoon every time your phone talks to you." Eliana giggled.

I laughed. "That might help me with my withdrawals." I shrugged. "I'll probably send him an email after school, just to see if he really does want to keep in contact. If he doesn't, he won't respond."

We reached our Spanish class and took our seats on the third row. But all through Mrs. Frederick's lesson I couldn't get my mind off of British Boy and the possible reasons behind his absence today. I really hoped our conversations hadn't been meaningless to him. I'd told him some pretty sensitive things about myself and thought we had a good thing going for us.

I set up an anonymous email account and sent British Boy an email as soon as I got to my car after school.

To: britishboy@awesomemail.com
From: mysterygirl@awesomemail.com

Sad we couldn't meet today. I was really looking forward to talking to you after last time. If you ever want to talk again just email me back.
– Mystery Girl

BY THE TIME I got home from watching Eliana's soccer game, I had an email from British Boy waiting for me.

I felt terrible not being able to meet you today. I'd love to keep in contact. -British Boy

It was a short email, but I couldn't keep the smile off my face, knowing he still wanted to be friends.

I responded back with: *I'm glad. Have a great night.*

My phone immediately pinged with an instant message from British Boy. I smiled at the thought of him wanting to talk with me some more.

BritishBoy: *How was your day?*

MysteryGirl: *It was good, aside from getting stood up by this guy with a gorgeous voice.*

BritishBoy: *The scoundrel. You're too good for him anyway. ;)*

I laughed. It was fun being able to joke around with him like this. I'd never been able to joke around with Noah when we were dating. Not that me and British Boy were dating or anything. I didn't even know his real name.

MysteryGirl: *It's ok. Eating my lunch in the dark was getting tricky anyway.*

BritishBoy: *At least you were smart and brought your lunch. I bet the poor schmuck was just hungry today.*

MysteryGirl: *Maybe. Got any fun plans for the weekend?*

BritishBoy: *Not really. You?*

MysteryGirl: *Working on a project with a guy from school. It's probably going to take most of the day.*

BritishBoy: *Sorry. I hope he's at least tolerable to be around.*

I thought about my last couple of interactions with Luke. He was definitely becoming more tolerable these days.

MysteryGirl: *He's cool. Has a bit of a rebellious streak, likes to joke around a bit too much. I used to think he was really annoying, but I don't know about that anymore.*

BritishBoy: *Sounds like you know him well.*

MysteryGirl: *Actually, not really. He's surprising me more and more.*

FRIDAY NIGHT, I went to the movies with Eliana and Jess since I didn't have to dance at the out-of-town football game. Jess broke up with Stacy yesterday after school, claiming that

Stacy was becoming too clingy for him, so it was just the three of us.

"How are things coming along with the dancing competition?" Eliana asked, as we waited for the movie to start. We were sitting in our usual seats in the very back row. The theater was crowded tonight with couples and teens excited to see the latest thriller.

I took a sip of my soda to wash down my bite of popcorn. "It's going fine. Luke did okay at our last practice. I'm still trying to decide exactly what I want to do with our dance. I'm sure it'll come to me once I pick a song. Lucky for me, we're free to do whatever style we want."

Jess offered his box of Junior Mints to Eliana and then to me. "You don't think he signed up for this just to have another way to prank you, do you?" Jess asked.

I shook some candy into the palm of my hand. "I don't think so. He hasn't told me why, but it seems like there's a personal reason for it."

Something like understanding dawned on Eliana's face. "That's right. I remember my parents talking about his mom last year and how her cancer had come back again."

"His mom has cancer?" I asked. Did everyone have cancer these days? Why hadn't he said anything when I was at his house?

Eliana nodded. "Yeah."

Maybe that was why no one was at his house on Wednesday. Maybe she was bedridden? Or in the hospital getting treatments? There was a heaviness in my chest as I thought about how hard that must be for Luke to deal with right now. He was in high school. He wasn't supposed to be worrying about his mom possibly dying.

I pushed those thoughts away. "I hope the dance competition

helps keep his mind off things. It's always nice to have a distraction when things are hard."

The theater lights dimmed and the last people found their seats. Jess leaned closer to Eliana and whispered just loud enough for me to hear, "Did you guys ever decide what Ashlyn has to get you since you won the bet about my sad dating life?"

I groaned internally because I just remembered what I was going to have to do.

Eliana looked slyly at me before turning back to Jess. "We actually agreed to make this one a little different than the other times. Instead of her buying me something, she gets to wear her pajamas to wherever I choose. It's pretty much going to be awesome."

Jess gasped. "Ashlyn is going to wear her pajamas in public? I have to see that."

Eliana grinned. "I'm just trying to decide where I'm gonna make her go. I did think about having her walk around the mall tomorrow night, but somehow that doesn't seem nearly humiliating enough."

A sneaky smile spread across my brother's lips. Sometimes sharing a best friend with my brother was not the best. "I heard Jake Haley's throwing a party next Saturday. You should totally make Ashlyn go there. Might teach you guys to quit this betting game of yours."

I felt the blood drain from my face. "No way. I will not go to a party in my pajamas."

"Oh, but I think you will." Eliana laughed. "And I was thinking those footie pajamas you got for Christmas last year might be the perfect outfit for the night."

12

LUKE

"WHO HAVE you been texting all night?" Kellen called across the aisle to me. It was ten p.m. on Friday and we were driving home on the bus from our game against Cortland High. We'd won twenty-eight to fourteen, and everyone was feeling pretty good about it.

"Just some girl I met," I said, hoping he'd leave me alone. Messaging with Ashlyn was actually a lot of fun. She was witty and smart, and after texting her constantly for the past few days, I was starting to regret not getting to know her better sooner.

Kellen leaned over to get a closer look. I pushed the side button to make the screen go dark. I wasn't about to let him find out that I'd been pretending to be some British dude.

Kellen raised his eyebrows. "Oh, so you're sending *those* kinds of messages. I totally get that." He held up his knuckles for a fist bump.

I shook my head. "No, we just talk."

Kellen's eyes widened in disbelief. "Just talk?"

"Yep. Some girls like a little conversation."

Kellen shrugged. "Not girls I'd be interested in."

Yeah, Kellen was definitely not the kind of guy who would just message a girl.

Noah turned in his seat. I hadn't realized he was sitting in front of me until that moment. "You're messaging with some chick? Telling her all about your *feelings*?" he taunted.

I ignored him and looked out the window at the street lamps we were passing.

Noah continued, "That's all Ashlyn ever wanted—to talk about her feelings. Never wanted to give it up for me. Glad that's over."

I clenched my hands into fists, resisting the urge to punch Noah in the face. But I didn't say anything because I wasn't supposed to know what he'd done to her.

My phone vibrated with another message.

MysteryGirl: Don't ever make a bet with your best friend over your brother's relationships. You will regret it.

BritishBoy: Why do you say that?

Why would anyone gamble on Jess's relationships? He went through girls faster than even Kellen and Jake...and he was a nerd.

Mystery girl: I may or may not have to wear my pajamas to a really public place next weekend.

That was not something I ever imagined Ashlyn would say. I didn't think I'd ever seen her not looking her best at any time. She looked spectacular even in her dance workout clothes.

BritishBoy: I wish I could see that.

MysteryGirl: You could if you wanted.

That made me smile. That meant she liked me enough that she wanted to meet again. Too bad that was the last thing we'd be able to do.

BritishBoy: If only we hadn't set up the ground rules of not revealing too much about ourselves.

Ok, if Noah or Kellen saw those last few messages, their dirty minds would totally read them differently. I peeked up just to make sure they weren't. Thankfully, they were both talking to Jake about his party.

MysteryGirl: Rules are meant to be broken sometimes.

BritishBoy: We'll see. But not yet. I'm liking our deal way too much. But maybe someday.

I just hoped she wouldn't slap me when that someday came.

MY PHONE RANG late Saturday morning, waking me up. My hand fumbled around my nightstand, trying to silence it.

Who was calling me? My mom was the only person who had ever actually called me. Everyone just texted.

I blinked my eyes a few times and they eventually focused enough to read the name on the screen.

Ashlyn Brooks.

"Hello?" I said the word slowly, the phone pressed against my ear.

"Hey, Luke. Did I wake you?"

"Uh, no," I lied. I tried to quietly clear my throat.

"Good." She sounded relieved. "I just had the best idea for our practice. Are you free for a couple of hours?"

I frowned. "Depends."

There was no telling what Ashlyn might come up with.

"It'll be fun. I was thinking about our last practice and I came up with the perfect way to get you to loosen up." Her voice was bright, and I could just imagine the big smile on her face.

"What are we doing?" I asked cautiously.

"It's a surprise."

I shook my head and chuckled. "That sounds dangerous coming from you."

She laughed. "No one will be harmed. I promise."

"How reassuring."

"You're going to love it. Pick me up at one o'clock?"

My dad would be out golfing most of the afternoon, which left me alone in my empty house. I had actually been looking forward to my dance lesson with Ashlyn today, since we were becoming pretty good friends already, even if she didn't know it. But the surprise she had up her sleeve worried me. From our pranking war, she definitely had a great track record for humiliating me.

I looked out my door to the hall. Empty. I listened to the sounds of my house. Silence. And I knew my answer. I'd do almost anything to feel normal again. And these days that was most likely to happen with Ashlyn.

I sighed. "I'll be there."

That afternoon, I drove to Ashlyn's house without the slightest clue of what we might be doing.

She must have been watching for me from the window, because as soon as I parked against the curb, she opened the door. She sashayed down the steps wearing a lacy yellow dress that looked amazing next to her bronzed skin in the sunlight. I tried not to let my mouth hang open as I watched her. Her legs were long and toned, and she looked way too good for me to be alone with for a few minutes, let alone however long we'd be together this afternoon. She looked beyond hot. She was breathtaking.

I tried to wipe the admiration off my face as she climbed in the Jeep.

"If I would've known you were going to wear that, I would've worn more than just a T-shirt and shorts," I said as she buckled herself in.

"So you like it then?" She looked up at me through her eyelashes. Had her eyes always been such a beautiful shade of blue?

I swallowed. "Don't pretend like you don't know what a dress like that does to a guy."

She gave me an appraising look. "You look great too, Luke. And what you're wearing is perfect for today."

She directed me to Syracuse, which was about a twenty-minute drive. What would have normally been an uncomfortable ride with a girl was surprisingly enjoyable. I'd never had such an easy time talking to someone before—well, except for when I talked to Ashlyn in the dark and through our messages. I'd assumed it was because she didn't know who I was and that I didn't have to worry about being judged. But now, I was starting to think it was just because Ashlyn had something special about her that made me feel like I could tell her anything. She even laughed at my jokes, which didn't always happen with high school girls.

"Now that we're almost there, can you tell me where we're going?" I asked as I pulled off the freeway into Syracuse.

She shook her head and there was mischief in her eyes. "Not yet. Before we can do that, we need to stop by a store."

She directed me to a shopping mall a few blocks from the exit and told me to wait in the Jeep while she ran inside. A couple of minutes later, she came out holding these huge panda head things that I could only assume were supposed to go on top of our heads. She opened the door and climbed into the Jeep with a big smile on her face.

"Don't these look so fun?" she asked.

"I thought we were going to be dancing, not dressing up for Halloween."

"Why can't we do both? Halloween is next month, after all. Plus, I promised today's experience would be a lot of fun, right?"

She'd said that all right, but I didn't think I was going to like Ashlyn's version of fun very much. "And where are we going to wear them? We're just going back to my house, right?"

"Of course not. I wouldn't have you drive us all the way here if that was my plan." That sneaky smile of hers spread across her lips. "We're going to entertain the residents of Syracuse this afternoon. Give them a show to brighten their day."

Pretty sure whatever show she had planned would darken mine.

"And where are we doing this?" I asked.

She pointed out her window to the street corner next to a stoplight. "Right there."

I didn't say anything. I couldn't say anything. All I could do was sit there with my heart pounding out of my chest. "We're standing on a corner wearing panda masks? How is that supposed to loosen me up for dancing?"

"We won't just be standing there. We're dancing."

I turned the key in the ignition. There was no way I was going to do that. "We're leaving. Right now. I'll just tell Max we can't do this thing."

"You don't think that sounds fun?" She pouted like I'd just hurt her feelings.

"Why would I ever think that sounded fun?"

"Because it will be with me." She grinned, and I almost believed her. "I'm known for being a lot of fun, didn't you know that?"

"Nope," I said, hoping she'd give up and change the plan.

"Just think of it this way, Luke." She turned to face me, her expression serious for the first time since coming out of the store. "No one will recognize you. I brought you to Syracuse so you wouldn't have to worry about any of your friends or neighbors seeing you. You can learn to dance in front of a crowd but not have to worry about what they'll think of you, because they'll have no idea who you are. Just give me fifteen minutes, and if you're not having fun after those fifteen minutes we can leave."

I put my hand on the key, still debating whether to leave or not. I sighed and looked at the panda head she held out to me. It was huge, and you couldn't really see inside it at all. Maybe my identity would be safe.

"Okay. You've got fifteen minutes."

As soon as I climbed out of the Jeep, I put the panda head on. Ashlyn did the same, leading me to the street corner. I couldn't help but notice that she had a certain skip in her step. I had no idea how she could be excited about this, but somehow, she was.

"Okay, Luke. Just do what I do and try to remember to have fun while you're at it." Ashlyn's voice came from inside her panda head.

"I'll try." Though I doubted I would have any fun. This was going to be humiliating.

We got to the busy street corner, and there were all kinds of cars driving down the road past us. This wasn't one of the quiet residential roads in Ridgewater that I was used to. Instead, it was bustling and busy, and I wondered if everyone in Syracuse happened to be in their cars at that moment. I looked longingly back to my Jeep, seriously considering if I should just run and leave Ashlyn behind. But she had promised me only fifteen minutes. I could survive that long. There were definitely worse things she could make me do.

Ashlyn turned on the music on her phone, and pretty soon, the *Chicken Dance* song was playing from the Bluetooth speaker she'd brought with her.

"Are you serious?" I asked Ashlyn.

"We have to loosen you up somehow. This is one of the simplest dances I could think of. They tell you exactly what to do." I couldn't see her expression, but I was pretty sure she was enjoying this a little too much.

I just stood there with my arms crossed as Ashlyn began flapping her arms, wiggling her butt, and clapping her hands. How could she be so fearless? It didn't seem like anything could scare her.

"Do it, Luke. The time doesn't start until you actually dance."

I sighed and flapped my arms at my sides like a fool. A couple of cars honked at us. And when I looked up, there were kids in the silver minivan just ahead laughing their heads off at my ridiculous performance.

But as the song went on, I slowly loosened up. And by the time the song ended, I was actually kind of having a good time. Maybe Ashlyn didn't have the worst ideas in the world.

DANCING on the corner in Syracuse ended up being more fun than I'd expected. And the panda heads did make me feel a lot less self-conscious of my bad dance skills. I could now claim to be a professional at the *Chicken Dance*, and if the *Watch Me* song ever made a comeback, I could totally *whip and nae nae* as good as the next guy.

It'd been fun to see people in their cars smiling at us as we danced, little kids laughing from the backseats. The only person who didn't enjoy our performance was an old man driving past with a huge scowl on his face. But maybe he hadn't actually looked at us, because we were awesome.

"It's kind of like we just did community service," Ashlyn said as we walked back to the Jeep, her panda head tucked under her arm.

"Definitely. If I ever get in trouble with the law, I'll be sure to tell them that I've already served my time."

She nudged me in the side. "You had fun. Admit it."

I couldn't keep the smile from my face. "Fine. It was kind of fun." I twirled the panda head in the air. "Maybe we should wear these for the competition."

"I'll keep that in mind."

We drove back to Ridgewater. I pulled up to the curb in front of her house. "Any fun plans for the rest of the weekend?" I asked, not wanting to say goodbye yet.

"Not really. Probably just going to hang out with Eliana and Jess. Might go to the mall."

"Chic Girl Boutique having a sale?" I grinned—it was a reference to the "boyfriend wanted" ads I'd made.

She shook her head. "How did you even know that's my favorite store? There's no way I ever told you that before you put it on those posters."

I shrugged. "It just seemed like your kind of place. Plus, I might have seen you coming out of there one day last summer with bags looped all the way up your arms."

Her face went red. "I promise it's not like that every time. They had a really good sale that day."

I held my hands up and laughed. "I wasn't judging."

"Good." She smiled, her hand on the door handle. "I'm gonna try to figure out our dance this week, so I don't think there'll be much for us to practice until I get the choreography nailed down."

"So no practice then?" I asked, trying not to feel too disappointed.

"I thought you'd be happy about that."

I shrugged. "I don't know. Dancing isn't as bad as I thought. In fact, I might almost call it fun."

She laughed. "Don't worry. Once I get it figured out, you'll be spending most of your free time with me."

My chest lightened. "If that's what winning this competition will take, I'm willing to suffer through it."

She rolled her eyes. "Well, be careful what you say, because I still have the ability to make it as painful a process as I want."

I sobered. "Please no tights. I promise not to complain about anything, as long as you don't make me wear tights."

She grinned, probably enjoying making me squirm, but she said, "Fine. No tights."

I blew out a breath and relaxed in my seat. "I'm going to hold you to that."

She smiled. "Well, I better let you go. I'm sure I'll see you at school on Monday."

I nodded. "Yep. Have a great rest of your weekend. Don't spend too much money at the mall."

13

ASHLYN

I SET the panda head on my dresser after getting home. Hanging out with Luke had turned out to be a lot of fun, and watching him get more comfortable with dancing was rewarding. He was tall and awkward, but it was kind of cute in a ridiculous sort of way.

But now I had to go back to the drudgery that was Saturday homework. I may have faked needing tutoring lessons to keep Luke from finding out about British Boy, but the sad truth was that I probably needed a tutor for real. There were so many names and dates to memorize, and I totally bombed the last quiz. I thought I'd done a good job, but apparently, Mr. Phipps didn't want a description of what happened over two hundred years ago in my own words. He wanted me to just memorize what the book said and write it down word for word. It was ridiculous. I even studied for hours for this quiz.

I tried to focus on my History textbook, but my mind kept wandering to what British Boy might be up to. After reading the same paragraph five times in a row and still not knowing what I'd read, I decided that my grades would just have to wait until later.

As if he'd read my mind, my phone beeped with a message.

BritishBoy: How did your project go today?

MysteryGirl: It was good. Turned out a lot more fun than I thought it would.

BritishBoy: That's always good.

MysteryGirl: Yeah, we still aren't even close to finished, but I don't think it's going to be nearly as bad as I thought it would at first. My partner is turning out to be cooler than I originally thought.

BritishBoy: Good for you. I love it when things like that happen.

MysteryGirl: Me too. Makes me wonder what it would be like if you and me ever got partnered together on something.

BritishBoy: It would probably be epic. The best partnership in the history of partnerships.

I smiled. He was too sweet. Which had me wondering...

MysteryGirl: Would you ever want to meet? Out of the Chem lab, that is?

I saw the conversation dots on the screen, like he was typing a response. My heart pounded as I waited for his answer. I still had no idea who he really was or what he looked like. But sharing the things we'd shared with each other had made me feel closer to him than I'd felt with anyone in a really long time.

After an agonizing few minutes, he finally responded.

BritishBoy: I think that would be nice someday. But I'm not quite ready to reveal who I am yet.

I sighed, disappointment washing over me. Maybe he didn't feel the same way about me as I did about him.

I decided to take the lighter approach to the situation though.

MysteryGirl: Waiting to have plastic surgery first?

BritishBoy: Haha. The only reason I'd need plastic surgery would be to make me less hot. I don't think you could handle my face in all its glory.

That made me smile.

MysteryGirl: I'll believe it when I see it.

BritishBoy: Ok.

I'd hoped he'd say more about why we couldn't meet yet. But he didn't.

There was a knock on my bedroom door—it was my sister Macey.

"Hey, is it okay if Taniah and I go to the mall with you guys tonight? Mom said we could go."

I slipped my phone into my pocket, deciding to leave my conversation with British Boy there for the moment. "Sure. We can go now if you want."

Macey's face brightened. "Awesome! I'll tell Taniah that we're on our way."

THE NEXT WEEK flew by as I tried to figure out exactly what song Luke and I should dance to. But nothing was coming to me. I listened to song after song on Sunday, but none of them had the right feel for us. Probably because I had no idea what we were anymore. After our panda-head bonding experience, we were definitely not enemies, but we weren't quite friends yet, either.

So instead of figuring that out, I ended up getting sucked into messaging British Boy in all my free time. His conversations were addicting, and I could only imagine what it would be like if we were talking in person. We'd already gotten past all the initial getting-to-know-you type of stuff and had moved on to discussing things I didn't even know about my own brother and sister. Aside from learning all about his favorite bands and political views, I learned about the little quirks he has, like how he sometimes eats popcorn with a spoon. And how he always has to put his right shoe on first.

Walking around school was weird now, because each new face that I saw held the possibility of that person being my secret pen pal. Anytime I sent a message to British Boy, I'd look around just to see who else might be on their phones at that exact moment. I'd actually followed a few guys around the school for a while, just waiting to hear them speak with a British accent. But so far, all that had gotten me was a few tardies and no actual insights in who British Boy might be.

"Have you figured out our dance yet?" Luke asked me on Friday during school. "I'm free to practice tomorrow morning if you want."

I groaned. "I've been so busy all week that I haven't had a chance." Busy. Distracted by British Boy. They were kind of the same thing.

"Busy with what?" he asked.

"Um, just stuff."

He tilted his head and gave me a look of disbelief. "What kind of stuff?"

I blushed under his gaze. I needed to get out of there before I ended up telling him about British Boy. "Just stuff. I promise I'll work on it this weekend."

"I hope so. Because we only have just over a month left, and I'd rather not embarrass myself too much in front of the crowd."

"It'll be fine. We'll practice on Monday. Okay?"

"I'll hold you to that."

I blew out a long breath as he walked away. I really needed to focus. But focusing would be a whole lot easier if British Boy wasn't so entertaining.

14

LUKE

MYSTERYGIRL: You need to stop being so fun to talk to. I'm totally neglecting my responsibilities.

I smiled when I woke up and found the message Ashlyn had sent me Saturday morning. When I'd asked about the dance, I had guessed I might be part of the reason behind her "busyness" with "just stuff," but this confirmed it. And I didn't know whether to feel proud or guilty because of it, either. Our conversations were really good, and I had also been ignoring my responsibilities because of them way too often this week.

BritishBoy: You could ignore me if you wanted.

MysteryGirl: That's the problem. I don't want to.

Which was my problem as well.

BritishBoy: You can always turn your phone on airplane mode. I can't distract you if you don't get my messages.

MysteryGirl: But then I'd just be distracted wondering what I was missing.

I laughed. I knew that feeling all too well.

BritishBoy: Fine. How about we set a timer? We can chat

for ten more minutes. Then we both have to promise not to message each other for the rest of the day.

It would be hard. But I could do it. I had Jake's party to keep me busy tonight anyway.

MysteryGirl: Deal.

It would be fun to see whose self-control cracked first.

15

ASHLYN

THE TIMER IDEA ACTUALLY WORKED. I still didn't get any of the choreography figured out, but I did get my homework done for the day. I figured I could worry about the dance tomorrow. I usually worked best under pressure anyway.

And there was no way I'd be able to concentrate on anything else when I had Jake's party looming over my head. I'd tried to talk Eliana out of making me wear my pajamas to it all week, but she wasn't budging. Apparently, she wanted to make her one time winning a bet count for all the times she'd had to buy me new accessories at Chic Girl Boutique.

I was just about to put on my pajamas when my phone beeped with a message.

BritishBoy: Got any fun plans for tonight?

I smiled, happy that British Boy had broken the rule we'd set for ourselves. Looks like I wasn't the only one who enjoyed our conversations.

MysteryGirl: Sadly, yes. And I'm totally dreading it.

BritishBoy: Because of the pajama thing?

MysteryGirl: Yep.

BritishBoy: I'm sure you'll look great.

MysteryGirl: Since you totally know what I look like.

BritishBoy: I can imagine.

Hmm. What did British Boy think I looked like? I was so curious.

MysteryGirl: What do I look like in your head?

BritishBoy: Pretty.

So descriptive. But it was nice that he imagined me as pretty. I could work with that.

MysteryGirl: And what does pretty look like?

He didn't respond for a minute, so I started changing into my pajamas.

My phone beeped again.

BritishBoy: Blue eyes. Blonde hair. Brilliant smile.

I frowned.

MysteryGirl: Did you somehow see me in the Chem lab?

I zipped up the front of my pajamas and studied myself in the mirror. I looked like an overgrown stuffed animal.

Maybe I should paint whiskers on my face, find some bunny ears, and pretend I thought Jake was throwing a Halloween party...one that was over a month early.

Why did I have to make these stupid bets with Eliana?

Probably because I usually won and that made them addictive.

I turned away from my reflection when a message came through from British Boy.

BritishBoy: No. Does that mean I imagined you correctly?

MysteryGirl: Maybe. Wanna know how I picture you?

BritishBoy: I'm dying to know.

I did a quick Internet search until I found the perfect photo. I sent him the screenshot, smiling to myself as I waited for his response. I only had to wait a second.

BritishBoy: You think I look like Quasimodo from the *Hunchback of Notre Dame*?

I texted back, laughing so hard I could barely type. Good thing autocorrect was my ally today.

MysteryGirl: I figured since you still don't want to meet that it must be because you look different from the normal teenage guy.

BritishBoy: Well, while my nose is slightly more pronounced than I'd like, I'm sorry to say that's where the similarities stop.

MysteryGirl: Sad. I was really hoping you had a huge bump on your back and interesting-looking eyes. That's totally my type.

BritishBoy: So you have a type, then?

I thought about all the guys I'd liked through the years. Most of them had been tall, since I didn't like the idea of being taller than the guy I was dating. They also usually had brown hair. I couldn't remember half of their eye color, but I did love a good golden brown.

Luke's face popped into my head. Which was weird. I'd never had a crush on him. Maybe his face came to my mind because I'd just been thinking about the dance competition?

I didn't know if I wanted to tell British Boy about my preferences toward guys. He already seemed self-conscious of his looks. Would he be less likely to meet if he didn't have brown hair and brown eyes?

But I decided to take a chance. My Biology teacher last year had told us that darker colors were dominant, so maybe I'd get lucky and say the right thing to British Boy.

MysteryGirl: Brown hair and brown eyes are my fav but personality trumps all that.

You could be the hottest guy in the world, but if you treated me like garbage, it was over. I'd definitely learned that lesson the hard way before and wasn't about to make the same mistake again.

BritishBoy: Then I might be in trouble.

MysteryGirl: Because of the brown hair and eyes, or personality?

BritishBoy: Personality.

So he was my type. Nice.

MysteryGirl: I don't think your personality is a problem.

I couldn't remember being attracted to a person's personality more than I was to British Boy's. I wouldn't have tried to meet him in the Chemistry lab a fourth time if I wasn't interested. And so far, all I had to go by was his personality. If he looked anything like he sounded, I'd be in huge trouble. There was about zero chance of me not falling head-over-heels for this guy.

He didn't respond for a minute. I'd probably caught him off guard with that, it was almost as good as admitting that I liked him. And maybe it was the bunny pajamas that made me feel like putting myself out on a limb, but I was suddenly feeling braver than usual and I wanted to put everything out there. I'd known him for less than a month, but already I felt closer to him than I had ever felt to someone.

MysteryGirl: Do you think it's possible to like someone you've never seen?

BritishBoy: Yes.

My skin went all cool and tingly at that one word. Was it possible that British Boy liked me too?

I GRABBED a quick dinner from downstairs after finishing my conversation with British Boy. My hands were shaky as I reheated a leftover vegan enchilada. I had told British Boy that I liked him, and instead of telling me I was nuts, he had hinted that he liked me, too. This was crazy!

But instead of staying home and daydreaming of the day I'd see his face for the first time, I had to go to a party looking like a stuffed animal. Stupid bet.

My mom walked into the kitchen. She gave me one look and her expression turned dark. "I thought you were going to a party with Jess and Eliana tonight."

"I am." I brought my plate out of the microwave and grabbed a fork from the drawer.

"Dressed like that?" Her tone made it sound like I was committing some sort of crime.

"Yes, Mom. It's going to be a long party and my pajamas are comfy," I said, just because I knew she'd hate it.

"Well, I never," she huffed. "I wouldn't dream of letting anyone see me in my night clothes." Yep, she wouldn't. She barely let our family see her without makeup on.

And even though I hated to admit it, I was a lot like her. Which was why tonight was going to be extremely painful.

I quickly ate my dinner, and then ran upstairs to put on my bunny slippers—I might as well complete the ensemble. I also grabbed a change of clothes and stuffed them into one of my bigger purses, in case Eliana decided to let me off the hook at some point during the night.

Jess knocked on my bedroom door a few minutes before it was time for us to leave. "You still think betting on my relationships is fun?" he asked with a smirk on his lips.

I slung my bag over my shoulder and strode past him. "Of course. Though, if you ended up dating the girl we all know you want to date, this whole betting game of ours wouldn't even exist anymore."

I looked over my shoulder to catch his reaction. He looked confused for a moment, and then understanding slipped across his features and his mouth formed an "O." But he didn't say anything, like always. Somehow, there was an unspoken rule that Jess and I could never talk about his admiration for our friend. But hopefully he'd get up the nerve one of these days.

Eliana was just coming out of her house as we drove up to the end of the driveway in Jess's lime green Camaro. I had opted to sit in the back, not wanting any onlookers to notice my outfit for the night. Eliana climbed in then gave me a good look over.

"This is even better than I thought," she said, her smile huge.

I crossed my arms and tried to give her a solemn look. "Enjoy it while you can, because this is never happening again."

"I wouldn't be so sure. Jess is bound to find a new girlfriend by next week." She smiled at my brother and nudged him in the side. "Am I right?"

Jess sighed and rolled his eyes. "We'll see."

His gaze met mine through the rearview mirror. The look in his eyes warned me to keep my lips zipped about him and Eliana ever dating—especially because Eliana was oblivious to Jess's real feelings and didn't seem bothered about his future dating life. I felt bad for my brother and hoped that someday Eliana would see what was sitting beside her.

We drove a few blocks away to Jake's two-story brick home and parked right in front since we were early.

"So I only have to wear this costume for fifteen minutes, right?" I asked Eliana before we got out of the car. She bit her lip and was quiet for a moment, as if thinking over just how much she wanted to torture me. But when a couple more cars pulled up, she turned back to me.

"I guess I'll be nice and let you off with just fifteen minutes.

Especially since Luke's here. He's bound to make those fifteen minutes worth every second."

I turned my head toward the opposite side of the street and saw that Eliana was right. Luke was climbing out of his Jeep, wearing a navy blue T-shirt and a pair of dark denim jeans. I should have known he'd be here.

Hopefully he'd remember how well we'd bonded during our panda head dancing and not use tonight against me.

We walked up the steps, and I made sure to keep my bag close to my side, hugging my change of clothes like it could shield me from all the strange looks I was about to receive. Luke quickened his pace as he ran across Jake's lawn and stepped in line with me.

"When I decided to come to this party tonight, I had no idea this was the treat I was in for. If I'd known you were such a fan of bunnies, I would've used them in my pranks last spring."

My face flushed with heat. "Just remember that we're friends now and that putting anything on YouTube as some sort of prank might have dire consequences for you and any future dance lessons you might have."

He grinned. "I'll have my camera ready."

We made it to the front door. Jess was about to knock when Luke pushed the door open and led us into the house. There were already a few girls standing around, talking to Jake and Kellen and a few other guys on the football team. Jess and Eliana immediately gravitated toward the foosball table in the corner, which was unoccupied at the moment. And I was left to stand beside Luke.

Luke leaned closer. "Do you have to wear that the whole night?" he asked, probably noticing my panic at the sudden attention I had. Jake and Kellen, who had been giving a rendition of something that had happened at the football game the day before, suddenly stopped mid-story and stared at me. The three girls surrounding them noticed their stare and turned to look at me.

Hannah Evans gave me a smirk. "Did somebody tell you this was a costume party?"

I wanted to turn invisible. "I lost a bet."

"I'll say you lost something. Don't know if it's a bet, more like your sense of fashion. You actually sleep in those?"

I looked down at my feet, wishing I hadn't added the slippers to the ensemble after all. I looked totally ridiculous.

I was still trying to think of a response when Luke slid his arm around my shoulder and said, "Actually I think your pajamas are hot. Pretty sure all guys do. Reminds them of some other bunnies. Am I right?" He raised his eyebrow at Kellen and Jake who then nodded obediently.

Not that I wanted to be compared to the bunnies Luke was hinting at, but it was a nice gesture anyway.

"You want to get something to drink?" Luke leaned his lips closer to my ear, sending chills racing down my spine. "Jake usually has soda and water in the kitchen."

I nodded, grateful for the excuse to leave the room. My cheeks cooled as we entered the spacious kitchen with its ceiling-high, cream-colored cabinets and an industrial-size fridge that could hold enough food to feed an army—or Jake and his four brothers.

Water bottles sat in an ice cooler beside the kitchen island. Another cooler held a variety of sodas. I grabbed a Dr. Pepper and popped the top.

"Thanks for standing up for me in there," I said.

Luke grabbed a water bottle and shrugged as if it was nothing. "I gotta stand up for my dance partner...even if you do like to torture me a little too much."

"You had fun last week, and you know it." I grinned at him.

"It was okay. Not sure I'll ever do that again. But it was fun for a one-time thing."

I checked the time on my phone. It was only five after seven. I still had ten minutes to go before I could get out of this ridiculous outfit. I wondered if I could go find an empty room upstairs and hide out. Eliana and Jess seemed to be distracted enough by their game. I didn't think they'd notice if I went missing.

That's how it always was when those two were together. Nothing else existed. It should probably make me jealous that they'd gotten so close to each other while I'd been dating Noah. But I couldn't be mad that my brother was encroaching in on my best friend. We had always been the three musketeers. At least I still got to hang out with them both after abandoning them last year.

Jake stepped into the kitchen, looking for Luke. "Hannah and Trinity don't believe that you can sound just like Gollum. Want to help me out and prove them wrong?"

Luke set his water on the counter and turned to me. "I better go settle the score." He checked the time on his watch. "Think you can endure the next ten minutes without me?"

I laughed. "You go ahead. I'll be fine. Thanks though." I wondered how I'd never noticed before how thoughtful Luke was. Probably because in the past, he never let me get to know this side of him. We were too busy having a war with each other.

A few more people came to Jake's party, their voices reaching me in the kitchen. I looked around, wondering if there was someplace I could hide before anyone else saw me. It sounded like the living room was filling up.

I peeked around the corner and saw that Jess and Eliana were still into their game. They probably wouldn't even notice if I went and changed right then. So, I grabbed my bag and left through the kitchen's back exit. There had to be a bathroom around here somewhere.

I was walking down the carpeted hallway when someone barreled out of the bathroom and almost right into me. I stepped to the side just before we could collide.

"Hey, watch it." A gruff voice growled.

I recognized the voice and ducked my head down, hoping its owner wouldn't look very closely at me.

"Is that you, Ashlyn?" Noah asked.

I considered ignoring him and just running into the bathroom. Instead, I met his gaze. His brown eyes were looking me up and down, and he had a cut that looked somewhat fresh on his cheek.

"Oh, hi Noah," I said, hoping to play off the sudden anxiety in my chest. "Great party, huh?"

He stared at me for a minute, apparently stunned that I'd shown up in my pajamas. "You didn't think this was a slumber party, did you?"

"It's not? Man, do I feel dumb."

"You should. It's not your best look. It looks like you've let yourself go. Has your mom stopped preparing your specially-made salads for you to eat every day?"

My stomach turned to stone. Had he really just said that? "I lost a bet, okay?"

He raised his eyebrows. "You sure did. And it looks like you're here all alone. I definitely wouldn't want to be seen around you. In fact, I'm gonna leave you here right now. Can't have anyone thinking we're getting back together. I have my reputation to protect." And he left.

I disappeared into the bathroom and locked the door behind me, leaning against the wall to try and calm my breathing.

THE SUN WAS JUST BEGINNING to set behind the trees as

I made my way out onto the back patio at Jake's house. There were a few chairs sitting around the table, but they were right in front of a big window and I didn't want anyone to see me sitting alone outside. I wanted to hide from the world after what Noah said. I wanted to leave. But as much as I wanted to leave, I didn't have the energy to go looking for Eliana and Jess. Where were they?

There were steps in the backyard that led onto the grass, so I sat down and pulled out my phone. Hopefully British Boy could help me feel better again, like he usually did.

MysteryGirl: High school is stupid. Remind me to never go to another party again.

I leaned against the railing and looked up at the sky. It was turning shades of purple and pink, and the moon was just peeking up from behind the houses and trees.

My phone vibrated in my hand. Thankfully, British Boy was easier to find than my friend and brother.

BritishBoy: Did something happen?

MysteryGirl: Ran into my ex-boyfriend. He's a real piece of work. But he also has a special talent of making me feel like garbage.

BritishBoy: Give me his name and I'll punch him for you.

I smiled. British Boy always knew just what I needed to hear.

MysteryGirl: He's pretty big. And I'm sure he fights dirty.

BritishBoy: I could take him.

I couldn't help but wonder if maybe that was true. I had imagined British Boy as a lanky type of guy—more like the guys in all those old British shows. The fine gentleman wearing their three-piece suits at all times and drinking tea with the queen. But maybe British Boy wasn't like that at all. Maybe he was tall and strong and lifted weights in his free time.

An image of Luke flashed into my mind again. I didn't know

why I kept picturing him as I talked to British Boy. But apparently, my mind thought Luke would make a good protector in this kind of a situation. He'd already stood up for me once tonight.

But I didn't like the idea of British Boy getting into a fight. I had already dated the aggressive type, I didn't need to like another boy with a temper.

MysteryGirl: It would probably be better if the earth just swallowed me up.

BritishBoy: I beg to differ. If it did, I wouldn't get to talk to you anymore. That's kind of the highlight of my day.

I smiled. British Boy really was the sweetest. If we ever did meet, I'd probably throw myself at him. I shook those thoughts away. That would be weird. And I really didn't want to scare him off.

I was just about to respond to his message when I heard the back door open. I turned to look over my shoulder. Luke was coming outside, his gaze sweeping around for a moment before his eyes met mine. *Had he been looking for me?* His soft footsteps walked to my hiding spot. I stuffed my phone in my pocket, not wanting him to see that I'd been messaging someone named British Boy.

"I was wondering where you went," he said. "Looks like you decided to change your clothes."

I shrugged. "Yeah, I'd leave the party if I could. But I can't find my ride."

His brow furrowed. "Why do you want to leave?"

I sighed, not really wanting to get into it. But he seemed sincere, genuinely wanting to know. "Noah was being a jerk. He kind of ruined the party for me."

Luke lowered himself down beside me on the step. "I'm sorry about that. If it makes you feel any better, he totally got creamed by one of the football players on the other team last night. It was awesome."

He smiled, and I couldn't help but smile back. "Shouldn't you be mad that your teammate was tackled? Aren't you like the team captain or something?"

He shrugged, his shoulder rubbing against mine because we sat so close. "I probably should care. But you're not the only one who dislikes Noah. There's just something about that guy that rubs me the wrong way."

"Tell me about it." I rolled my eyes.

Luke didn't say anything for a moment, and when I looked up, he seemed to be studying me. It was as if his brown eyes were searching for what I wasn't saying about Noah.

"Did he treat you badly then?"

I averted my gaze and nodded. "You could say that."

"Was it like...bad stuff?"

I sighed. "Nothing like you're probably thinking. He never physically hurt me. I guess you'd call it more like emotional abuse. He was really manipulating too."

"Was he like that the whole time you were dating?" Luke asked.

I thought about it. I wasn't sure if I really wanted to get into it. The only other person I'd said anything about this to was British Boy. I just didn't like talking about Noah—it made me feel stupid for having even dated him in the first place. But it hadn't started out like that.

He'd been sweet at first, and really charming.

"It started out great. But then when things started changing at his house, he started changing, too."

I covered my mouth, realizing I shouldn't have said that about Noah. He didn't like people knowing that his stepdad had issues.

"Please don't tell anyone I said anything. Noah doesn't want people to know."

Luke shrugged. "I won't. I'm pretty good at keeping secrets."

The way he said it made me wonder if he had a few of his

own. I still didn't know a lot about Luke, but I hoped that we had become close enough of friends that he would be comfortable letting me get to know him better. But when he didn't say anything more about whatever secrets he held, I decided to change the subject.

"So, did you end up impressing everyone with your Gollum voice? I never knew you were good at different voices."

He seemed to grow uncomfortable under my stare. He looked to the side briefly before saying, "It's a weird talent. Not one I like to use very often. It's more embarrassing than anything, really."

"Does this mean you're not gonna show me your Gollum impersonation?"

"Yeah, probably not. I don't typically do that one in front of cute girls."

Cute girls? Did he just say I was cute? I didn't know how I felt about that. Sure, Luke was obviously good-looking himself. But I never really thought of him in that way. I'd never thought he'd think anything of my looks either. He was the football captain after all. He had all kinds of girls trying to date him. It was strange to think he might have noticed anything about me.

16

LUKE

I DIDN'T KNOW what I had expected Ashlyn's reaction to be after I said she was cute. I guess I hadn't expected any kind of a reaction at all, since I hadn't planned to say that. It slipped out. I could have tried talking my way out of it, but I decided to let it sit. She *was* cute, and even though British Boy was initially trying to get Ashlyn to fall in love with him, I was the one who was actually having feelings. And that was unsettling. I hadn't liked a girl for a really long time, and I probably wouldn't even know what to do anymore.

"Wanna get out of here?" I asked when the silence had stretched on long enough to make me feel awkward.

She looked at me with question in her eyes. "Don't you want to stay? Aren't you, like, the life of the party?"

"Not anymore. That was the old Luke. New Luke doesn't really fit in with his friends now."

"And why is that?"

I didn't know if I wanted to get into it. But, maybe it would be good if I did.

"I guess the new Luke has changed a lot since his mom died.

So it's harder to joke around and be the life of the party when no one seems to understand what I'm going through." I pinched my lips shut. Why did I say that? *Way to be a downer, Luke. Now she's totally going to want to hang out with you.*

"Your mom died?" she asked in a soft voice.

I had assumed she didn't know, from the way she'd acted with Mom's photos at my house. But her response confirmed it.

"It happened this summer. She had cancer."

She swallowed. "I'm so sorry, Luke. If I'd known, I would've never done half the things I did to you. I feel like such a jerk."

"Nah, it's okay. I actually liked having the pranks for a distraction. They gave me something to do." I turned to her with a guilty expression. "Though it probably wasn't very nice of me."

"What kind of cancer did she have?"

"Breast cancer. This was the second time around and her body was just too weak to fight it off for much longer."

"That's terrible. I can't even imagine." Ashlyn leaned against my shoulder and looped her arm through mine. The gesture was so simple but meant more to me than she could ever know. Someone cared about me. She cared.

It took me a moment to speak, but when I could, I said, "Thanks. It's been a long couple of months."

"Will you tell me about her?"

I hadn't talked to anyone about my mom for a long time. I didn't know if I could. But I wanted to. I missed her so much, and maybe telling Ashlyn about her would help her stay alive in my heart a little better.

"She was awesome," I started carefully. "She worked part time at my dad's law office and did everything you'd expect a mom to do. When she was well, she came to all my football games. She was my biggest fan and sometimes even argued with the refs when they made a bad call. She loved to cook and sing and dance." I gave Ashlyn a sideways glance. "Which is another reason why I couldn't say no when Max asked me to do the dancing thing."

"She sounds wonderful."

"She was." I winced, hating that I was talking about her in the past tense.

"Is your dad home much?"

I shook my head. "No, he works a lot. I think that's his way of coping."

"Does that mean you spend most evenings alone then?"

"Yep. At least the ones when I don't have a game or dance practice." I gave her a half smile.

She frowned. "That's a lot of time alone. I'd go crazy."

Yep. That about summed it up, though I'd noticed that since I'd been messaging her as British Boy and spending more time with her, my crazy moments hadn't been surfacing as much. It was like Ashlyn was some secret ingredient to my sanity.

"Does your dad know how much time you spend alone?" she asked.

I shrugged. "I don't know. He probably thinks I'm hanging out with my buddies, goofing around like I used to. I was always a lot closer to my mom than to him."

"I'm sorry to hear that."

"It's okay most of the time." And when it wasn't, I went running. "Sorry, I was supposed to be cheering you up, not telling you my sob story."

Which was probably my cue that things would get awkward between us from now on. Instead of seeing me as this aloof prankster, I was now this sad lost puppy who was always on the verge of having a panic attack.

She studied me for a moment. "I can see what you're thinking," she said. "And no, I'm not going to treat you any differently, so don't think you get to tell me all this and have me feel permanently sad for you." Her lips lifted up into a smile, and I knew she was joking. Just the fact that she could joke with me right now made me feel immensely better. "In all seriousness though, Luke. If you ever want to talk about it, you can talk to me. I'm a pretty good listener, and I know what it's like to think you have no one to talk to. Maybe we can both do that for each other."

I nodded, and the anxiety that had built up in my chest dissipated. "I think I'd like that."

I probably liked that too much.

"DO you still want to get out of here?" I asked Ashlyn. It was dark now and there was a slight chill in the late September air.

"Yeah, let me just text Eliana and Jess so they aren't worried."

We got in the Jeep and ended up at Emrie's Frozen Treats, a new ice cream shop that I hadn't been to before.

As we were walking in, I realized how we probably looked to onlookers. We were a couple of high school students, wearing nice clothes, walking into an ice cream shop on a Saturday night. It was like we were on a date. Did I want it to look like we were on a date?

Probably.

Emrie's was decorated in the typical 50's style, complete with black-and-white checked tile flooring. The waitress seated us in the back corner booth that was fire-engine red. I immediately felt like I'd gone back in time. Instead of TVs everywhere, there were black-and-white photos on the walls and a sign that said, "No WiFi. Try talking to your date for a change."

"My mom would have loved this place," I whispered.

Ashlyn gave me an understanding smile, and I was once again so happy that I'd told her about my mom.

When the waitress came by again, I ordered a chocolate shake and Ashlyn ordered a vanilla.

"I never pegged you for the vanilla type," I told her after the waitress had left our table.

"I only pretend to be wild." She winked.

I laughed. That was definitely not true in my experience with her so far. Ashlyn was anything but plain old boring vanilla.

"So tell me more about yourself, Luke. We've been at Ridgewater High together for a couple of years, but other than our epic Food's class last year, I really don't know much about you."

She had no idea just how wrong she was. She knew practically everything about me.

"I'm not that interesting. Just a regular guy, going to school, playing football. Dancing in a competition." I laughed at that last part. Definitely not normal. At least not for me.

"What are your plans after this year? Are you going to college?"

"Yeah, I'm hoping to play football somewhere. Coach has scouts lined up to watch me play in a couple of weeks."

"If you could choose any school to go to, where would it be?" she asked.

I shrugged. "I don't know. My mom and dad met at Cortland State, so that's always been high on the list. But if I can play football, I'll go anywhere."

"Cortland State is my top choice, too!" She smiled. "Jess and Eliana both want to go to Cornell, so I figure it's close enough that we could still hang out on the weekends."

"You and your brother seem to get along well for being so close in age."

The waitress brought our shakes to the table. Once she was gone again, Ashlyn spoke, "We get along most of the time. But we do have our moments. What about you and your brother? Are you close?"

"As close as we can be. He's in the Army right now so we mostly Skype and talk about football." The Skype calls had become much less frequent since Mom passed away. It was like she was the glue that had held our family together, and now that she was gone nothing seemed to fit anymore.

"Wow, I really admire anyone who can do that. Your family must be so proud of him."

I nodded. "Yeah. He's the selfless service man. I'm the block-headed football player."

She frowned. "Why do you say it like that? You're in high school. You're doing what you're supposed to. Plus, you're really good at football...not that I've watched you that closely on the field," she hurried to add. Was she actually blushing? I'd never believe it if I hadn't seen it with my own eyes.

"I understand if you couldn't keep your eyes off me two weeks ago. I *was* looking really hot out there."

She snorted. "I'm pretty sure most people would describe it as icy-hot."

"You know that's an old joke now, right?"

"Whatever. I still have guys texting me over those boyfriend-wanted posters you put everywhere, so I might as well say as much as I can about that. I still don't think we're quite even."

"You've obviously never had Icy Hot put on a jockstrap before."

Her eyes twinkled. "Can't say that I have. And I don't think I'll be trying it out anytime soon."

"So you say you still have guys messaging you, thanks to my awesome posters. Anyone you're interested in?"

Was it obvious that I hoped her answer was no?

Her face flushed again. She looked down at the table. "There's this one guy. But I can't really give you credit for matching us up even if we did meet that day."

Uh, oh. She was about to tell me about British Boy. This was dangerous.

Just play it cool, Luke. "Who is it? Is he going to be mad that we're together?" My knee bounced under the table as I waited for her answer.

"No. At least I don't think so." She blinked her eyes shut briefly before looking back at me with an embarrassed expression. "I actually don't know who he is."

I tried to act surprised, but I was totally freaking out inside. *Alert. Alert. Do not proceed with this conversation,* my sense of self-preservation told me. But my curiosity didn't care about self-preservation. If she was going to talk about British Boy, I wanted to hear about him.

"Are you, like, online friends?"

"Something like that. We actually, um, met in the dark Chem lab on the first day of school. I was having a really bad day."

"No thanks to me." Why had I ever thought those "boyfriend wanted" posters would be a great way to start off the school year?

"Not just you. Noah, too. Anyway, he was really nice, and we sort of bonded in the dark. Now we just message each other, but I don't know...he's amazing." She sighed. "I've never met anyone like him before."

Her words warmed my insides, but they also worried me. If she was this smitten by my invisible persona, how would she ever see past him to the real me? After getting to know her better, I wanted her to want the *real* me. Not a guy with an accent. I could obviously just come out and tell her that I was British Boy. But I doubted our new friendship was strong enough to survive the possible betrayal she'd feel. She might say she's totally vanilla, but I could tell that she was full of fire, and I didn't want to risk getting burned.

So I just smiled and nodded. "He sounds great." Then I took a sip of my shake before I could say anything that would mess everything up. I needed time to think and figure out a plan. I'd gotten myself into this mess and it would take time and a lot of luck to get myself out of it.

17

ASHLYN

THE NEXT MORNING, I woke up and remembered that I'd never responded back to British Boy last night. Hopefully he wasn't worried about me—I had ended our conversation with talk of me wanting to be swallowed up into the earth. Thanks to Luke, I no longer felt like that.

I pulled out my phone and sent him a quick message.

MysteryGirl: Sorry I didn't get back with you last night. Something came up.

More like *someone.* But I didn't want British Boy to be worried about nothing. Luke and I were just friends...right? But it was getting more and more confusing the more time we spent together. He was turning out to be a lot different than I'd thought, and if I didn't already like British Boy I might have found myself texting him instead of British Boy this morning.

BritishBoy: Did you stay at your party?

MysteryGirl: No.

I hesitated to tell him about what actually happened. I didn't want to make him jealous. But it wasn't like British Boy and I were dating. I still didn't know what he looked like. In fact, maybe telling him that I was hanging out with another guy would actually help our relationship move forward. People always liked the chase, so maybe if I suddenly wasn't as available to British Boy, he might want to meet again. And I needed to meet him. I needed to figure out if there was anything between us besides a bunch of conversations.

So I messaged him back.

MysteryGirl: Remember the guy I was working on that school project with? He came to my rescue and we hung out. He's pretty cool.

BritishBoy: Sounds like a nice guy.

I wished I could tell what those words really meant. Were they supposed to be encouraging, or was there a slightly jealous tone to them?

MysteryGirl: He is really nice. Pretty cute, too.

I giggled to myself. Hopefully, British Boy would react the way I was hoping.

BritishBoy: Cute, huh? Do you like him?

I could interpret that as jealousy, right? But then again, maybe not. I wished I could hear his tone when he said that. Was this even going the way I wanted? Should I make it sound like Luke and I were more than friends?

My shoulders dropped as I blew out a frustrated breath.

Maybe this was a dumb idea.

MysteryGirl: We're just friends.

BritishBoy: But do you want to be more than friends with him?

Was this his way of testing me somehow? What was the answer that would make British Boy want to meet me again?

MysteryGirl: I don't know.

Did British Boy want me to be more than friends with Luke? Was he trying to tell me to go after him so that he didn't have to worry about me liking him anymore? Had I scared him when I told him I liked him, and now he was desperate to push me onto someone else? I really had said that super quickly. We did just barely meet a few weeks ago. He probably thought I was crazy!

I read over the messages again, but I still couldn't figure him out. So much got lost in translation between our phones. This would be so much easier if we were having this conversation face to face. Then I could gauge his facial reaction or listen to the tone of his voice.

Maybe I should just change the subject.

MysteryGirl: What did you do last night?

It took a moment for him to respond.

BritishBoy: Hung out with a good friend.

Good friend? What did that mean? Was his good friend a girl, or was his good friend a guy? I wanted to ask him but knew that it would just make me sound jealous. So I tried to go for the cool approach.

MysteryGirl: That's fun. It's always great to hang out with friends.

BritishBoy: It is. She's great.

She?

She!

MysteryGirl: Your friend is a girl?

Breathe. Don't panic.

I wiped my hands on my pants as I waited for his response.

He'd just said good friend. Not *girlfriend.* There was a big difference between the two. No need to get worried.

After a few agonizing moments, my phone beeped.

BritishBoy: Yeah.

I threw my phone on my bed.

This wasn't fair. British Boy shouldn't be able to meet other girls and make friends with them. He was supposed to only want to spend time messaging me.

But that was exactly what was wrong with our friendship. We had a barrier between us, keeping us from becoming more than just pen pals.

I needed to figure out a way to fix that. Soon.

I picked up my phone and shoved it in my pocket, deciding not to message him back right now.

To get my mind off British Boy and his possible future girlfriend, I decided to be productive and spend the rest of the day choreographing the dance Luke and I would do together, using my little sister as a stand-in for Luke. I picked the song *A Thousand Years* by Christina Perri. I'd already taught Luke the basic waltz step, so hopefully he'd catch on to the choreography quickly enough. A month wasn't a lot of time to learn a dance, especially since we were both really busy with school and our extracurricular activities. But I picked the slow song with hopes that it would be simple enough, while still looking elegant.

I tried to relax that evening, but I couldn't stop thinking about who British Boy's good friend might be. What if she was really cute? What if their friendship turned into something more? I knew from my own brother's friendship with Eliana that it was extremely possible for British Boy's friend to want more from their relationship...especially since he was so amazing. I hadn't even seen him and had already fallen fast and hard.

But sitting around and worrying wouldn't do me any good, so I decided to give my brain a break and watch a movie instead. I texted Eliana to see if she wanted to join me.

Eliana: **My grades are gonna die if I don't do my homework tonight. Watch one of those BBC movies you love just for me?**

Me: **Ok, I'll totally daydream that Persuasion is really about British Boy and me. I think someone wrote a letter in that movie. It's kind of the same.**

Eliana: **Totally, plus that guy is way dreamy. Blond hair. Captivating eyes. *Sigh***

Maybe she should look at her blond-haired, green-eyed best friend a little more closely if she had a thing for Rupert Penry-Jones. Jess could totally pass for a younger version of that guy.

I went into the kitchen to pop some popcorn. Macey and Jess were sitting at the table, playing a game of Boggle.

"Practicing up so you can finally beat Eliana?" I asked Jess as I walked by.

He shrugged and scribbled down a word. "Maybe."

While waiting for the popcorn to stop popping, I pulled out my phone to check my text messages. A thrill of excitement went through me at the thought of British Boy messaging me again until I realized we didn't send texts. Just messages through the awesomemail app.

I opened the texts anyway—there was one from Noah and another from Luke. I ignored Noah's.

Luke: **I'm so bored that I actually want to work on our dance today. Did you finish choreographing it?**

I checked the timestamp. It was sent over three hours ago. I felt bad that I'd missed it. Hopefully he hadn't been lonely and sad all day.

I quickly texted him back.

Me: **Just got your message. Was in the zone choreographing our dance earlier. Just about to watch a movie, if you want something to do that doesn't involve dancing. I'll warn you though, it's a chick flick.**

His text came back less than a minute later.

Luke: **Chick flicks are better than my empty house. Just got back from a run. Be right over after I shower.**

I smiled, happy that I'd done something nice for him.

The popcorn was finally done, so I mixed it with melted butter and my favorite seasoning. While I waited for Luke to arrive, I opened the text from Noah, hoping it wasn't another insult.

Noah: **Sorry I was rude yesterday. I didn't mean what I said about you letting yourself go. You caught me at a bad time. My stepdad was on one yesterday and I took it out on you.**

I sighed. I didn't want to feel bad for Noah. It was the same as it had been when we'd been dating. His stepdad would do something, and then Noah would take it out on me. The cycle needed to end somewhere.

Me: **Sorry about your stepdad. But that doesn't mean you can be a jerk to everyone else.**

Noah: **I know.**

The doorbell rang, so I left our conversation there. Noah would need to figure things out on his own this time around. But it was nice that he apologized. That was something new.

When I opened the door, Luke was standing on the doorstep, wearing a green button-up shirt with dark blue jeans. I didn't know if it was the sunlight streaming behind him or what, but he looked really good today. He was always handsome, but somehow, he looked even better than usual.

Was it a bad sign that I liked British Boy but also thought Luke was cute?

I blinked my eyes, pushing the thoughts out of my mind. Luke and I were just friends. Just like British Boy and his good friend, who happened to be a girl.

"Come on in, Luke. The theater room is back here." I smiled to cover my awkwardness.

He stepped inside and looked around the house as we walked down the entryway and past the kitchen.

I opened the door to the theater room and flipped on the light. I gestured to the various recliners and couches. "You can pick a seat wherever."

"And what chick flick are we watching today?" Luke asked as he settled down onto a reclining loveseat in the middle of the room.

I gave him a half-smile. He was going to hate this. "I talked to Eliana earlier, and she suggested the perfect movie for the mood I've been in lately."

"And what is that?" He set his arm along the back of the couch, curiosity on his face.

"It's one of those old BBC movies. I've been going through this British kick. There's just something about the regency time and the accents that gets me every time."

An uncomfortable look crossed his face but it was gone an instant later. "My mom loved watching those movies when she was sick. Will you think I'm less manly if I admit that I've watched pretty much every one of those?"

"Not *that* much less manly." I grinned at him as I pulled out the DVD case from the shelf. When he made a face, I said, "I'm kidding. That's actually really cool. I mean, obviously I like them as well."

"Yeah?"

"Don't they say real men wear pink? It's kind of like that." Plus, Luke definitely looked manly with those broad linebacker shoulders of his.

He laughed. "Just don't tell my buddies, okay?"

I put the DVD into the player, grabbed the remote, and sat beside Luke on the loveseat.

"Speaking of British stuff, is there a new guy from England on the football team? I'd heard something about that."

He looked startled for a second, but his expression smoothed over a moment later. "No. I don't know of any English guys on the football team."

Dang it. I guess British Boy wasn't on the football team after all. Maybe that guy at the game wasn't his dad like I'd assumed.

The movie started, and I realized the room was still bright.

"Sorry, I forgot to turn off the lights." I scooted forward in the seat to stand.

Luke reached over and grabbed my arm as if to stop me. "No, that's okay."

"Are you afraid I'm gonna try to put the moves on you? Because you're safe with me, Luke. I know we're just friends."

He furrowed his brow. "No, it's just that I, um, have a hard time watching movies in the dark since my mom died. It's mostly what we did the last days before she passed away and it takes me right back there." His face was so open and vulnerable. He looked younger somehow.

My heart broke for him. How had he gone through something like that? It wasn't fair. His mom had died before his senior year of high school. It wasn't supposed to happen. She was supposed to be sitting on the bleachers, cheering him on as he made a touchdown. Not watching him from heaven. It almost made me want to cry.

"We can do something else if a movie is too hard," I said in a soft voice.

He shook his head. "I have to start watching movies again sometime. I'd rather try it with you than when I'm alone."

I watched his face carefully to see if he really meant it. He looked like he did, so I said, "Okay, but we'll leave the lights on."

He smiled gratefully, his brown eyes holding mine. "Thanks."

I scooted closer to him, hoping it would be more comforting

than awkward for him to have me be so close. He stiffened for a second, as if caught off guard by the gesture, but then he slid his arm around me and pulled me closer to him. I had planned on it being a quick hug, but when he seemed to relax and breathe deeply, I decided to stay. Hugs had always been healing for me in the past, so maybe I could try to help him heal from his heartache.

I never would have believed it a week ago that I'd be cuddling with Luke Davenport while watching a romantic movie. Never in a million years. But it was kind of nice. He felt nice. Right somehow. I wondered if it would feel this good to cuddle with British Boy.

When Captain Wentworth appeared on the screen, looking gorgeous in his old-fashioned clothing, I imagined British Boy walking toward me when we finally met out of the dark. He'd stride into the room, wearing a nice tailored suit, perhaps with a cravat tied around his neck. He'd offer me his arm, and we'd go on a long walk in the countryside. Then when it was time for me to go home, he'd helped me into his carriage, and the simple touch of his hand would send waves of electricity through my whole body. He'd say goodbye in his dreamy, accented voice, and then I'd swoon while gazing into his brilliant brown eyes.

An image of Luke wearing a cravat popped into my mind. I shook the thought away. Luke was not British Boy. And it was not the early 1800's. British Boy probably had a car and regular clothes—though they were probably made from the finest material.

I sighed and focused back on the movie. I wished they still made love stories like they used to. This movie was so good.

"How are you liking it?" I asked Luke a while later.

When Luke didn't respond, I tilted my face up to see if he was still awake. He was looking straight ahead at the screen, his jaw working, and a tear trickling down his cheek. Luke was crying?

"Thinking about your mom?" I hugged his torso tighter for a second.

He nodded and wiped at his eye. "Yeah. It's just hard knowing I won't see her again."

"Let me turn off the movie. This was a bad idea." I moved to push myself away from him so I could stand, but his arms tightened around me.

"No. I need to do this, even if I look like a big baby."

I shook my head and wiped the tear from beneath his eye. "You don't look like a baby, Luke."

"I sure feel like one. This is humiliating."

I sat up and took his face in my hands so he had to look at me. "Your mom died. That's not something you just get over. If you weren't sad, I'd wonder what was wrong with you."

He stared back at me with his beautiful eyes and slowly nodded. "Okay, but I still feel stupid. This is exactly why I never talk about my mom with anyone."

"Don't feel stupid." I touched his shoulder. "I like it when a guy isn't scared to show his real feelings. It's refreshing." On impulse, I leaned closer and kissed his cheek. His skin was soft and smooth under my lips. It felt nice.

I pulled away slowly, shocked that I'd done that. When our eyes met, there was surprise in his, but there was something else there too.

Before I knew it, Luke had slipped his hand to the nape of my neck and was pulling my face closer.

My heart hammered in my chest. He was going to kiss me!

But at the last second, I turned my head away, and his warm lips brushed against my cheek instead.

"Sorry, Luke," I said, pulling away. "I can't kiss you."

His eyes were wide with disbelief. He shook his head, as if

trying to orient himself. "Did I read everything wrong? I thought..."

Oh man, I had given him all the wrong signals. I'd cuddled with him, kissed him on the cheek, had him watch a romantic movie. Of course he'd interpret those things into me having feelings for him.

"We're just friends. I'm sorry if I made things confusing, but I like someone else."

His brow furrowed. "Your pen pal?"

I bit my lip and nodded, feeling horrible after everything he'd told me today. He'd opened up about his difficulties getting over his mom, and I was here pretty much giving him a slap on the face.

But I didn't like Luke that way. British Boy was the guy who occupied my thoughts when my head rested on my pillow at night.

It probably sounded ridiculous that I was falling for someone I'd never even seen. But I had fallen for British Boy. I needed to see things through with him. Yes, Luke was really cute and surprisingly sweet, but we were just supposed to be friends.

"I really like him. I can't kiss you and message him at the same time. That wouldn't be right."

He took my hand in his. "But you shouldn't worry about that, Ashlyn. I don't know how to say this, but I'm—"

He stopped when his eyes caught on something behind me. I turned my head and found my sister standing in the doorway.

"Can I watch the movie with you guys?"

Thank you, Macey, for saving me from this super awkward conversation.

"Sure, join the party." I waved her in.

Hopefully, Luke and I could forget about what had just happened and never talk about it again. It was only because he was emotional that he'd tried to kiss me. When we were both thinking straight, and I'd had a chance to talk to British Boy again, our new friendship could go back to normal. There shouldn't be a reason for us to get all awkward around each other. I hoped.

Though I'd be totally lying if I didn't admit that a small part of me wished I hadn't turned my head.

But I'd ignore that part for now. It was just a tiny part, anyway.

18

LUKE

WHY DID her sister have to come in at the exact moment I finally gained the courage to tell Ashlyn the truth? Instead of getting to explain myself, I had to sit through the rest of the movie looking like a rejected fool who had gotten her cheek.

Her cheek!

Who does that?

Apparently, me—a guy who couldn't differentiate a pity cuddle from a real one.

But maybe it was a good thing that I hadn't been able to tell her I was British Boy. Knowing Ashlyn, she would have slapped me instead of telling me to forget the awkward cheek kiss and give it another try.

But I knew I needed to figure out how to get British Boy out of the picture. Just having Ashlyn nestled under my arm for most of the movie had been amazing. I really wanted to do it again, soon. I just needed to figure out a way to tell Ashlyn the truth.

We finished the movie around seven. I went home right after having another totally awkward conversation about how she knew I was emotional and that I wouldn't have tried to kiss her if I'd been myself.

Feeling about as humiliated as I could get, I decided not to correct her and just let her think she was right. Someday I'd figure out how to tell her everything.

When I got home, I was surprised to see my dad standing in the kitchen with a tall red-headed woman I didn't recognize.

"Hey, Luke," my dad said when he noticed me. "I'm glad you're here. I wanted to introduce you to Amy."

The woman, whose back had been turned to me, swiveled around and looked at me with a nervous smile. I didn't like that smile. It told me I wasn't going to like the reason why we were being introduced.

My dad gestured to the bags of food on the counter. "We grabbed some dinner from Alessandro's on our way here. Let's have a seat and talk."

My dad wanted to sit and have a talk with me? He'd barely even seen me over the last two months, and now he wanted to talk with an audience? But the food did smell delicious, so I grabbed one of the to-go boxes off the counter and sat at the dining room table. My dad and the woman had a whispered conversation before joining me. I took a bite of the pasta on my plate. Alessandro's had the best food. I didn't even know what this was called, but it was good.

Dad cleared his throat. I wanted to ignore him and whatever he had to say, but when he cleared his throat again, I looked up.

"I guess I should probably start by telling you who Amy is." My dad fidgeted with the fork in his hand. "She's been working at my office for a while. And I wanted to introduce you to her."

Amy from dad's office. My stomach shriveled up. She probably wasn't just a friendly coworker.

"Hi, Amy." I shoveled a forkful of pasta in my mouth so I wouldn't have to say anything else.

"Your dad has told me so much about you, Luke."

I swallowed down some water before saying, "That's funny, he never said anything about you." I glared at my dad. I knew what was coming.

"Amy and I have something to tell you."

This better not be some twisted way of telling me I had a new mom or something.

"We have started dating." He said the words slowly as if expecting for me to explode. He might as well have kicked me in the chest.

"Dating?" What did that even mean?

"You see, Amy and your mom were really good friends before she passed. So after she died, Amy was there for me, to talk about your mom and share the memories I had. And soon we were sharing even more."

My chair screeched along the tile floor as I scooted away from the table. I couldn't sit and listen to this. My dad was telling me that he'd betrayed my mom on her deathbed. How long had this Amy really even known my mom? Had she just seen my mom's death as a ticket into my dad's life and money?

My heart started beating fast and my head started pounding. It felt like my chest was being stepped on, I could barely draw in a shallow breath.

It was happening again. Another panic attack. I had to get out of here.

I was out the door and running before my dad could say anything else.

And I kept on running and running and running.

I ENDED up at the park just down the street from Ashlyn's house. I hadn't gone in that direction on purpose. It seemed my subconscious thought she was my safe place. But there was no way I could let her see me like this after she'd turned away from my attempted kiss earlier.

But I wished I dared knock on her door and talk to her right now. She always knew how to make me feel better even after I'd turned into a crybaby this afternoon.

I did a few pull-ups on a bar and had a stroke of genius.

I couldn't have Ashlyn knowing that *I* was turning into some crazy guy, but maybe British Boy could. I needed her to stop liking him anyway, so if she thought he was messed up in the brain, maybe she'd want to forget all about him and finally be able to see me as more than the immature prankster she'd initially known. British Boy wouldn't look quite so charming if she knew he was mentally unstable.

I pulled out my phone and messaged Mystery Girl.

BritishBoy: Do you ever feel like you're losing your mind?

MysteryGirl: Sometimes. Why?

BritishBoy: I feel like I'm going crazy a lot. I just found out that my dad has a new girlfriend.

MysteryGirl: And I'm guessing that's not a good thing?

Of course it wasn't a good thing. But she had no idea that British Boy's mom had just died. Or Mum, I guess, since that's what they called their mothers in England.

BritishBoy: Not a good thing, even if my mum isn't in the picture anymore.

I couldn't say that she had died or that would totally give everything away. Hopefully she'd assume they were divorced or separated or something instead.

MysteryGirl: Sorry to hear that. Wanna talk about it?

BritishBoy: It's just kind of like a kick in the face that my dad would come home with a new lady so soon. Like, doesn't he miss her at all?

MysteryGirl: Dads are dumb sometimes. And I'm sorry you don't like his girlfriend.

Yeah, I didn't really know her of course, since I'd run out the door almost as soon as we were introduced. But she wasn't my mom.

She'd never be my mom.

MysteryGirl: Do you think we should meet in the Chem lab? I'd love to talk to you in person about something.

She wanted to meet? I paced around the playground as I tried to figure out what to do.

There was only one thing I could think of that Ashlyn would want to talk to British Boy about, something that she couldn't discuss through our instant messages. She wanted to talk about her feelings. It had to be that. But if I was ever going to get British Boy off her radar the way that I wanted to, he needed to disappear. And even though it would be so much easier to have British Boy just ghost her and not meet with her tomorrow, she deserved to have it done in person. British Boy would remain a gentleman and handle this delicate situation the best he could.

He was going to move back to England. That was the only way for a clean break. If he was an ocean away, there was no chance of anything happening between them and Ashlyn would eventually realize that they weren't meant to be after all.

It wasn't the most honest thing in the world, but it was the only way possible to keep both versions of me from losing her. And I couldn't lose Ashlyn. She was my lifeline to sanity.

So I messaged her back before my conscience could talk myself out of it.

BritishBoy: Tomorrow at lunch?

MysteryGirl: Yes. Meet me there.

Hopefully this whole mess would be over with by tomorrow at twelve thirty-nine.

I WAS both nervous and excited all the next morning. Excited that I was almost done with my double life. But nervous that something would go wrong. Something seemed to always go wrong these days.

I left my second period class a few minutes early just so I could make it to the Chemistry lab before Ashlyn. If this was going to work, she could not see my face. I waited by the doors for the bell to ring since the lab was occupied that period. As soon as it was empty and Mr. Sawyer had turned out the lights, I snuck into the room. In all my thoughts about what might happen today in the lab, I decided I needed to be physically differently than the other times we'd been together. If she were to give British Boy a goodbye hug or something, I couldn't have her recognizing anything familiar about me. So I grabbed the hoodie I'd borrowed from my dad's closet out of my backpack and pulled it over my head. I had also made sure not to wear my usual cologne—instead I'd sprayed some of my dad's cologne on his hoodie this morning just in case she was the type to notice that.

I only had to wait a couple of minutes for Ashlyn to walk in the door wearing her scarf. I probably would have laughed if I hadn't been so nervous.

"Are you in here?" her voice cut through the silence once the door had shut behind her.

I blinked my eyes and focused on my British accent. I hated doing this to her, but it was the only way I could see out of this mess that I'd made. I just needed to make a clean break.

"I'm over here," I called to her.

Her footsteps clacked on the tile floor. She was probably wearing heels. She looked good in heels.

I shook my head. I wasn't here to think about how she might

look today. I was here to get her to move on and forget about the version of me that she'd elevated in her head.

Her footsteps stopped a few feet away from me. "Say something again so I can find you."

"I'm straight ahead. I'm guessing just a few steps away." It was so dark in here. Which was good.

Her footsteps sounded again, and a second later, one of her hands brushed along my chest.

"Is that you?" she asked. She sounded almost breathless, like she was so excited to finally be close to British Boy again.

"You found me," I said, my heart pounding fast. She was too close. I wanted to step away from her and pull her closer at the same time, but that might give away that something was up. So I stood tall and drew in a deep calming breath as quietly as I could.

She stepped beside me and leaned against the counter behind us. She smelled amazing. Better than I'd ever noticed before.

Which probably could only mean one thing—she had a special perfume for guys she was interested in. I didn't want to think about why she'd never worn it around me before.

"It's so good to hear your voice again," she whispered. "It seems like it's been forever."

"Why are you whispering?" I asked.

She laughed loudly, her shoulder knocking against my arm as she did so. "I don't know. I guess I'm just nervous."

"Don't be. It's just me."

"Which is exactly why I'm nervous."

"I'm just a normal guy."

"I'll have to take your word for it. You still look like Quasimodo in my mind."

"Well, if that's what floats your boat, then imagine away." I laughed. "But for the record, I don't look like him. Not even close."

"You do seem taller, I suppose. And..."

Suddenly her hand was on my back, feeling along my spine. I stiffened. I hadn't expected her to be so comfortable in touching me. Good thing I'd had the foresight to wear a hoodie.

"Yep, no hunchback either. How tall are you anyway?"

Would telling her my height give too much away? It shouldn't. There were a few other guys at school my height, her ex-boyfriend being one of them.

"I'm six-three. So yeah, pretty tall."

"Tall is my favorite kind of guy," she said in a flirtatious tone.

"Along with brown hair and brown eyes?" I hoped by reminding her of what she'd told British Boy before that she'd somehow picture me in her head instead of some made-up fantasy. I should be the last guy she'd hung out with who met that description.

"Yep. Which you told me you have as well."

I nodded before remembering she couldn't see me. I cleared my throat. "Yep." *Okay, Luke. Enough with the ice-breaking. Time to break something else.*

But before I could tell her I was moving, she spoke.

"You're probably wondering what I wanted to talk to you about."

"Very curious."

She sighed, and there was a lot of emotion in that one sigh. "I wanted to talk about us."

"Us?" I asked. Yeah, I definitely should have gone first.

"You had to have noticed that I've been thinking of you in more than the secret pen pal sort of way, right?"

"Nope. Never crossed my mind."

"It didn't?" She sounded so disappointed, and I immediately wanted to take the words back. I didn't want to hurt her. Just redirect her.

"Okay, so maybe it did once or twice. But I'm—"

"Good," she said before I could add that I was moving. "I'm so glad we're on the same page."

"And what page is that?" I asked, cautiously.

"I'd like to think that we're moving toward something great."

"Oh, about that..." I swallowed, trying to muster the courage to move forward with my plan. *Just spit the words out, Luke. You can do it. Freedom is just on the other side of this conversation.*

"Have you ever thought about us dating?" she asked excitedly, before I could get my lies out.

"Honestly?"

"Of course."

"Not really." The lie tasted yucky on my tongue.

She was quiet for a moment, and again, I wanted to take the words back. But there was no way British Boy could be thinking about them dating if he was moving out of the country that weekend.

"Why wouldn't you want to date me? Is it because of your *good friend*?"

Okay, just run with this, Luke. Maybe this was the universe jumping in and guiding the conversation in the direction it was meant to go.

"Yes, I mean no..." I floundered as I tried to get control of my tongue. I breathed in a deep breath. "I think you're great. I just don't know if you're my type."

That sounded nice enough, right?

"Why am I not your type? Please don't say it's because you think I'm ugly. Because we can totally turn on the lights and let you decide from there."

"No!" I nearly shouted. "It's not that. It's just that I, uh, tend to like really high-maintenance girls. You know, girls who keep me guessing. I like their unpredictable moods. There's something thrilling about it that draws me in. You're just so nice. I want a girl who'll fight with me and maybe sometimes be a little rude. I love having a lot of drama in my relationships. A good challenge is preferred, and I think things would just be too easy between us."

Wow, who knew I was so good at spewing a bunch of garbage under pressure?

"That makes, like, no sense." Her elbow bumped against me as if she was crossing her arms. "You pretty much just said that things would be perfect between us. Why would you want things to be hard?"

"I, um," I fumbled. "I think I'm messed up in the brain. I like to make things difficult for myself. You probably wouldn't be interested in someone like that, would you?"

"Are you being serious?" She sounded so confused. "Because I can be mean, if you really wanted me to be. Though I don't think that's a healthy way to have a relationship. Maybe you should talk to a psychologist about that."

What? "Are you saying that because you really meant it? Or are you saying that to be mean to me because you thought it would make me like you more?"

She laughed. "I guess you'll just have to wait and see. Maybe you shouldn't write me off too quickly."

Okay, so that idea had crashed and burned. The universe actually wasn't very helpful after all. Time for take two on getting British Boy off Ashlyn's mind.

"I didn't mean that. I actually think you're great. The thing is..."

"Yes?" she asked when I paused, her voice full of anticipation.

My stomach twisted with guilt. How could I do this to her? Maybe I should just tell her the truth. If she hated me afterwards, it would be because I deserved it. This "getting Ashlyn to fall for a fake guy" prank had turned out to be the worst idea in the history of mankind.

But instead of manning up and telling her the truth, I let another lie slip out. "I'm moving back to England."

19

ASHLYN

BRITISH BOY WAS MOVING BACK to England?

"But you just moved here. Why are you going back?" I asked in disbelief, trying not to collapse to the floor.

How could this be true? Things were finally moving forward between us. I was actually standing inches away from him instead of sending messages to him through the air.

"My dad just got offered a raise with his old company. And we miss our family back home."

I shook my head, not wanting to believe it. "How long until you go?"

"Next week. It happened rather fast." He added that last part as if it was an afterthought.

"So this is like a final thing, then? You're really going to be moving all the way across the ocean?"

"Yes. That's why you can't feel anything for me. There has to be someone else at the school you like more than me. It's not like you're going to be brokenhearted when I leave, right?"

"Of course there's no one else."

"What about that guy you were hanging out with on Saturday? Didn't you say you might possibly want to be more than friends with him someday?" I never should've told him about Luke.

"We're just friends. I don't think of him that way."

"Why not?" He sounded disappointed that I wasn't falling for Luke? I thought he'd been just joking around with me earlier when he said I wasn't his type. But maybe he really didn't feel anything for me at all. The thought of that made me so sad. How could I feel so much for him and he feel nothing? It wasn't right.

But he was moving anyway. So I guess it didn't really matter how much I'd just embarrassed myself in front of him. In fact, I might as well put everything out there since there was no hope for any sort of future between us.

"I don't have feelings for anyone else because I can't stop thinking about you." There, I'd said it. I'd told British Boy exactly how I felt about him. There was nothing else I could say to be any clearer.

"But you can't have feelings for me. We haven't even seen each other."

"I know it doesn't make sense." I sighed. "But you can't tell me that you don't feel something. I'm not even touching you, and yet, I feel more alive than I've ever felt before."

I reached down and found his hand; it was rough and callused and strong. It felt amazing, like he didn't mind hard work. His fingers twitched, and I knew he felt something too. That was what encouraged me to hold onto his hand a little more, slipping my fingers until they interlocked with his.

"Do you still feel nothing?" I asked in a soft voice.

His hand tightened around mine for a split second before relaxing again.

"It feels nice. But I don't know if I'd say it's any different than holding someone else's hand."

How could that be possible? My whole arm felt lit up with electrodes. How could he not feel what I was feeling?

I stepped closer so I was leaning against his side.

"What about now? You have any reaction to being this close to me?

The quickness of his breathing told me that he was feeling something from this.

"No. Nothing."

He was lying. Why would he want to lie about this?

I pushed away from the counter and stepped to where I thought I was facing him. I let go of his hand and just stood there in front of him. I felt his minty breath on my hair and knew our faces were only inches away from each other.

"Still nothing?"

He sighed. "Not a thing."

"You're lying. There's no way you're telling me the truth right now." I reached up and moved my hands up his arms until my right hand rested over his heart. "Your heart is racing as fast as mine. Why won't you just admit that you feel something for me?"

"Because I'm not supposed to. I'm not supposed to get into a relationship with you." This was the most sincere he'd sounded in our whole conversation.

"Why not?" I asked.

"Because..." He sighed. "Because it will make this that much harder when I move away. You won't be able to forget me. I need you to forget me." His voice was shaky.

"Why would you ever want me to forget you?"

"I can't explain."

What was going on with him? The air was charged with emotion, and I could feel that he liked me as much as I like him. He was just holding back because he was moving and didn't want to start something that had no chance of a future. But I knew I'd regret it for the rest of my life if I didn't kiss him right now. I needed that. We deserved it. A stolen kiss in the dark would be the only way I could say goodbye to my sweet British Boy.

I lifted my hand from where it still rested over his heart and tentatively gripped his shoulders, pulling myself closer to him so my cheek rested against his. He sucked in a breath as if my touch both surprised and overwhelmed him.

"I know you're leaving, and there's nothing I can do about that," I whispered, my lips next to where I imagined his ear would be. "But you've made me feel things these past few weeks that I've never felt before. I just want one more experience with you."

And before he could push me away, or run out the door, I took his face in my hands and pulled his lips to mine.

He stood frozen at first, like he was shocked that I would kiss him, but then a moment later, his soft lips were moving gently and carefully with mine. I didn't know what I had expected, but it certainly wasn't this. British Boy's kiss wasn't hurried and rushed like the other guys I'd kissed in the past. His hands didn't try wandering to places I didn't want them to go. Instead, he made me feel like I was special, like we had all the time in the world to get to know each other better. Like we had more than just today to kiss. And suddenly, I knew these few minutes wouldn't be nearly long enough.

My lips became hungry at the thought that they were standing on borrowed time. They wanted more. I pushed my fingers into his hair, which was softer and shorter than I'd imagined. He wrapped his arms tightly around me until there was no space left between us.

My heart hammered so hard in my chest I was sure he could feel it through my ribs. I had never had a first kiss like this, never had a last kiss like this either. It was like I'd been transported into another world and only he and I were there. We were all that mattered. Kissing British Boy was all there was.

But he was moving away. This was his last week at school.

My hands stopped combing through his hair. I couldn't do this. I wouldn't let myself enjoy this kiss any longer. It had seemed like a great, romantic idea. A goodbye kiss. But my heart couldn't handle it like I'd thought. I liked British Boy. I really did. And the fact that this was the best kiss I'd ever had was heart-breaking because I wouldn't have it again.

Sadness swirled through me as I slowed my lips. Our time was almost up.

A sob started building up in my throat and I pushed myself away from him.

"I'm sorry. I-I shouldn't have done that."

Before I could say anything else, he bent down next to my ear and whispered, "That's the most alive I've felt in months, Ashlyn. But I can't keep up this lie anymore."

He didn't have a British accent this time. British Boy wasn't British? And he knew who I was?

My knees weakened, and I gripped the counter for support. British Boy had been lying to me the whole time?

I felt along the wall behind the cupboards, looking for the light switch. I needed to see who this guy was.

His strong hands gripped my shoulders from behind and pulled me against his chest. "Yes, I lied to you. It wasn't right, and I wish I could take it all back. But if you knew who I was, you never would have given me a second thought." His British accent was back.

"Who are you?" My ears pounded as adrenaline coursed throughout my whole body.

"Someone who doesn't deserve you." And then he let go of me and disappeared. I scrambled toward the door, hoping to catch a glimpse of him, but instead I rammed right into one of the lab tables and banged my knee.

Why couldn't he just use his real voice again? I thought as I hunched over and rubbed my knee. My brain was clear enough that I might have a chance at recognizing it.

It couldn't be Noah, could it? He was the only person I could think of that matched what he was saying.

But no, Noah wasn't as thoughtful as British Boy had been. He wasn't a good listener. He was a mean jerk who made my life miserable. Plus, I would have recognized the way he kissed me, wouldn't I? It'd been a few months since we last kissed, but I couldn't have forgotten that easily, could I?

Then I remembered the text he'd sent me yesterday. Was he really changing for the better?

No. I shook my head. British Boy was real. I'd just imagined him speaking with an American accent a second ago. I couldn't have been tricked so badly by him. He was a good guy, not a master of deceit.

I finally made it out of the lab, but the hall was empty. I rushed down the hall to see if he was down the next one. I caught a glimpse of a guy wearing a red jacket with the hood pulled over his head.

"Hey, wait!" I called as I started running, not caring how it looked to the other students standing against their lockers. But the hooded guy didn't look back. Instead, he started running too. The warning bell rang, signaling the end of the lunch period. And with the bell, the hall burst with life again. It was only a matter of seconds before British Boy disappeared into the crowd.

I'd lost him.

WHEN THE CROWD cleared and I still couldn't find him, I knew it was futile. British Boy didn't want me to know who he was. He hadn't wanted to ever meet out of the dark because he knew exactly who I was, and for some reason, that kept him from me. Was I not good enough for him?

I walked back down the hallway with my shoulders slumped, slogging one foot in front of the other. About halfway down the hall, something red caught my eye. It was the sleeve of a red hoodie poking out of the garbage can.

British Boy had thrown away the one thing I would recognize him by. A few students lingered but none looked my way, so I grabbed the hoodie out of the garbage. I hugged it to my chest and continued down the hall. British Boy had been real, but not real in the way I wanted. This red jacket was the last thing I had to help me figure out who he was.

I stuffed it in my locker and debated whether I wanted to go to Spanish after all. I really didn't feel like it. I wanted to go home and mope in the privacy of my own room.

Today was supposed to be a great day. It had started out great. I'd been able to meet British boy. Had kissed him even. That kiss had been off-the-charts amazing. But then the world slipped out from under my feet and I found out that everything had been a lie.

British Boy had lied to me from the moment we met. And had just kept on lying to me.

I took a deep breath before heading into my Spanish class. For all I knew, British Boy could be in there watching for me.

All eyes were on me as I walked in. I tried to ignore their stares as I took my seat across from Eliana. Mrs. Frederick was standing in front of the class, lecturing about something like conjugating verbs. But she couldn't hold my attention. Not today.

Eliana turned her head and whispered, "How was it? Are you and British Boy going to be seeing more of each other?" She sounded so hopeful and sure that everything had gone well. Which it had, until the last minute we were together.

I shook my head and looked at the board so Mrs. Fredericks wouldn't suspect we were talking. "I'll tell you about it later."

After class, Eliana and I walked to our lockers together, weaving our way through the packed hall. Wherever I looked, I thought I saw him. Tall guys were everywhere, many with dark hair.

"Did you notice if Noah was in the cafeteria during lunch today" I asked Eliana, hopeful that he had been. I didn't want British Boy to be Noah. That would have been horrible if he'd listened in on everything that I'd said about him to British Boy. Was that why he apologized to me yesterday about Saturday night? Because I'd told him how badly he made me feel?

Eliana looked thoughtful for a second. "I don't think so, but I wasn't looking for him. Jess was flirting with Breanna Murdock all throughout lunch so that kind of distracted me."

My brother. Why was he doing this again?

But my brother would have to wait until later. "So you don't remember seeing Noah then?"

She pinched her lips, as if she was picturing the scene one more time. "No. I don't remember seeing him or not. Why?"

"I have a feeling British Boy might be Noah."

Eliana gasped, and her face turned from confusion to shock. "You think Noah is British Boy? Why would you think that?"

"Because of some of the things he said," I said, switching out some of my books from my locker.

"I'm so confused. What exactly happened in there today?"

I stared at British Boy's red hoodie. "Well, first he told me he didn't think I was his type. Giving me a bunch of garbage about how we were perfect for each other but that he wanted a relationship that challenged him."

"He did?" Eliana said with all the shock that statement deserved.

"Yup. That ended up being a bunch of crap, of course, so then he tried telling me that he was moving to England."

Eliana frowned. "Oh no. I'm so sorry."

I lifted my hand, cutting her off from her sympathy. "But that ended up being a lie too—at least I think so. But anyway, I was devastated about him moving and decided to throw caution to the wind. So I kissed him."

"You what?" Her voice jumped up an octave and her mouth dropped. "How was it?"

I bit my lip, remembering the kiss and how amazing it had been. But then I remembered how it ended. "It was really good. Almost like we were made to kiss each other." I had the sinking feeling that maybe it was so awesome because maybe we'd actually done it before. But Noah could not be British Boy. He just couldn't be. "Anyway, the kiss was really, really good, but then after, he said my name and told me he'd been pretending the whole time—all this in an American accent."

Eliana was silent. Then she said, "British Boy isn't British? How could that be true? I thought you said he sounded like it."

I nodded and shut my locker. "He must be an expert at tricking people into thinking he's from England. He said that he started doing it because he knew who I was from the start and that I never would have talked to him as himself."

"Oh." Eliana nodded as if she understood everything now. "So that's why you think British Boy might be Noah?"

"Yeah, and I really don't want him to be." Though he had lived with his grandma in London before she died a few years ago, right after his parents divorced.

"Do you think British Boy was faking being nice the whole time?"

I leaned against my locker. "I hope it wasn't all fake. But now I'll never know. He did lie the whole time, whoever he is. I just hope Noah wasn't trying to get some sort of revenge on me and planning to secretly share my secrets with the world."

"I doubt that's what happened. I mean, you guys have been messaging for a while. He had a lot of chances to use some of the things that you told him, but he hasn't yet. I think you'll be fine."

If only my heart would be fine. I'd fallen for him so badly. Having it all taken away in a second was crushing.

"Where do you go from here?" Eliana asked.

I sighed. "I don't know."

20

LUKE

I WAS nervous and shaky the rest of the day after my lunch period with Ashlyn. I didn't think she had recognized my voice, since I'd made it come out more gravelly than usual. But if she remembered all the clues I'd given her before, anything about me doing vocal impersonations, it was only a matter of time before she figured out the truth. I just hoped that by ending the deception now, instead of continuing it, that she'd find a way to forgive me if she did find out the truth.

But I had to admit that a huge weight had been lifted off my shoulders now that I didn't have a lie to keep up anymore. I really liked her, and even if she hated British Boy, hopefully she'd still be able to be my friend.

She messaged British Boy during fourth period.

Tell me who you are, please. That kiss was amazing, and I need to know this wasn't just some big joke to you.

My insides warmed at the thought that she'd liked kissing me as much as I'd loved kissing her. But I couldn't respond to her. The messaging needed to stop now. The lying had to stop now. She needed to forget about British Boy.

I was distracted all through football practice, which left me wide open for Noah. He seemed to be in an even worse mood than usual and hit extra hard today.

"Get your head in the game, Davenport," Coach yelled when I took too long to get back on my feet.

I stood, shook out my shoulders, and waited for Noah to come at me again. I needed to focus on what I was doing. Coach had sent tapes of our games to a few college recruiters and a handful had shown interest in coming later this season. I had to be playing at my best. I rolled my shoulders back and bit down on my mouth guard. I had to make it through practice, and then I could worry about Ashlyn again.

I managed to make it through the rest of practice without getting pummeled again. Afterwards, I grabbed a number four with a frosty from Wendy's drive-through then hurried home to shower. Before everything had gone down between British Boy and Ashlyn today, we had arranged to practice our dance at her house this evening. Part of me wanted to chicken out and cancel on her, but I needed to be brave and face her. I couldn't let on that anything had changed for me today.

I drove to Ashlyn's house after showering and putting on my real cologne. My heart started racing as soon as she opened the door. When she smiled at me, images of that kiss in the Chemistry lab jumped to the forefront of my mind. Her lips on my lips. Her fingers running through my hair. It had been incredible. The kind of kiss that inspired songs and romance movies and all that other lovey-dovey stuff. I was going to have a really hard time keeping my lips to myself now that I knew what it was like to kiss her.

"We're just going to practice in the family room today. I hope that's fine," she said as she led me into her house. As I followed her, my eyes kept wanting to linger on the colorful leggings she wore. But instead of checking out her butt, I forced my eyes up higher and admired her hair, which was pulled into a messy bun sort of thing.

"Did you finish choreographing the dance then?" I asked, hoping to break the ice between us.

"I think so. I picked the waltz, since it was something you're already familiar with. And hopefully, it should be easy to learn with our limited time together." She looked like she normally did, unless you were paying attention to her eyes, which were sad. Disappointed somehow. Like the thing that had given them light and excitement was now gone. I wanted to punch myself at that thought, because I knew it was all my fault.

"The waltz is good." Not exactly a cool hip-hop, manly dance I'd been hoping for, but I wasn't about to complain. I didn't deserve to, after everything I'd done to this wonderful girl in front of me.

She turned the music on, and a song that I'd heard a few years ago started playing through the speakers. "Is this *A Thousand Years*?" I asked.

She nodded and gestured for me to stand in front of her. Guiding me into the correct position for the dance, she set my hand on her back. She held my other hand in hers, and my palms immediately felt sweaty with her touch. She smelled just as good as she had in the Chemistry lab and I had a hard time breathing. The memory of holding her tightly in my arms with her body pressed against mine popped into my mind.

But sadly for me, while I was having a hard time controlling my breathing around her, she didn't have any sort of reaction to me at all. I tried not to feel too bad that she still didn't seem to recognize me since I should be thankful for that.

"Okay, so first we will start with the basic waltz step again, just to get used to the rhythm, and then we'll work on a few turns, lifts, and dips. Overall, it should be really simple, and hopefully, judges will interpret the simplicity for elegance."

"If you say so." Though it sounded pretty complicated to me.

On her cue, we started stepping slowly to the song. It was a beautiful song, a very romantic one that I'd imagine being played at weddings.

We danced through the song a few times until the triple step was fully ingrained into my brain. I'd probably show up to football practice dance-running in three-four time if I wasn't careful. By the time we took our first break, I had learned a quarter of the choreography she had planned for us.

Ashlyn turned off the music and slumped down onto the couch, looking so disappointed and sad.

"Having a rough day?" I asked, sitting down beside her.

She pulled the throw pillow over her chest and hugged it. "You can say that. More disappointing than anything, I guess."

"Disappointed in my dancing?" I asked, hoping to lighten the mood.

A small smile flitted across her lips. "Your dancing is fine. It's just something else didn't go quite like I wanted today."

"Something at school?" I asked, still playing dumb.

She twisted in her seat to face me. "Yeah, you know that guy I was telling you about on Saturday? My secret pen pal?"

I cleared my throat. "Yeah. The one you really like?"

She nodded and picked at her cuticles. "We met today, and I found out he's been lying to me the whole time."

"Yeah?" I rubbed the back of my neck. An alarm was going off inside me, telling me not to continue with this conversation, but I was too curious about her thoughts.

"I guess it's not going to work out between us after all. I just feel so stupid for having fallen so hard for someone who wasn't even real." Her blue eyes were so open and vulnerable. I wanted to reach over and give her a hug.

"What do you mean 'not real'?"

She blew out a long, heavy breath. "You see, this whole time I thought I was talking to some guy from England. But it turns out that he was faking his accent. He's just some regular guy from school who knew who I was and decided to play me hard."

My stomach turned to stone. When she said it like that, I really did sound like a horrible person. "Are you sure he was trying to hurt you? Is it possible that he knew how amazing you are and just didn't think that he stood a chance?"

She shook her head. "Yeah, right. No guy would think I'm amazing."

I did. But I couldn't tell her that. She didn't like me in that way. "You're awesome, Ashlyn. And tons of guys at school would agree with me. I mean, you did have a bunch of guys texting you a couple weeks ago, right?"

That earned me a half smile. "Okay, fine. Some of your friends seem to think I'm hot."

"And I think you're awesome, too."

She looked up at me and touched my knee. "Thanks for saying that. You're a great guy, Luke."

I stared at her hand on my knee, wishing I could cover it with mine. But I knew she'd probably snatch it away as fast as she'd given me her cheek yesterday.

"Oh well." She sighed, tucking a piece of hair behind her ear. "That's enough moping around for one day."

I smiled. "Yes. Enough of that. I'm supposed to be the mopey one in this partnership."

She smacked me in the chest with her pillow. "Nope. You can't mope either. Not when we have a dance to finish learning." She stood and held her hand out for me. "Break's over. Time to teach you that lift."

I let her help me to my feet, the feel of her delicate fingers in mine never getting old. Instead of walking to the stereo to turn on the music like I'd expected, Ashlyn stepped closer and gave me a hug.

"Thanks for listening to me." She spoke next to my ear. "You always know how to make me feel better."

I returned her embrace, enjoying the smell of her hair as I held her close. "Anytime."

21

ASHLYN

IT WAS strange how just a ten-minute talk with Luke could make me feel so much better. I'd been completely lost and depressed all day, and then suddenly I felt happy again. It was like Luke had taken the same magic that British Boy had used on me.

The second half of our practice went much better. Luke was catching on a lot faster than I'd expected, and before long, he'd learned the first half of the dance.

Now I just had to teach him the lift and we could call it a day. Lifts were what really wowed the audience and would hopefully get us the winning points from the judges.

"I was thinking you should spin me away from you." I took his hand and ran through the move as I explained it. "We'll both do a little arm flair, like this." I stretched my arm out to complete the full extension and waited for him to do the same. "Very good. Then I'll turn back in before gracefully jumping with my arms around your shoulders, and then we spin."

"Gracefully jump?" he asked, like those two words didn't fit together.

"Yes." I rolled my eyes. "Like this." I took his hand and repeated what I'd just showed him, completing it by jumping with my arms around his shoulders in a way that should have propelled us into a graceful spin.

But instead of turning the way I'd expected him to, he stumbled, and we crashed to the ground with a thump.

Ugh. Luke's knee was bony.

"Are your muscles full of air and just for looks?" I stood and rubbed my butt where I'd landed on his knee.

"No, of course not." He just sat there rubbing his knee. "I wasn't ready."

"Coulda fooled me," I said, joking. He was seriously ripped, so not being ready was about the only reason why he'd collapsed under my weight.

"I seem to remember you referring to my arms as guns the first time we practiced. So, yeah. You know there's not just air in there." He held his arm up and flexed his bicep so I could see the huge muscled bump that it was, with corded veins poking out and everything.

Dang. I bit my lip. His arms were definitely not made of air. They were made from heaven itself.

He grinned when he noticed my admiration and dropped his arm back to his side.

"Wanna help me up again? My air muscles are too weak to do anything." He held his hands out like a helpless child.

I offered him my hand, which he took, and then he immediately yanked me back down. Before I knew it, he had me pinned beneath him and he was tickling my sides.

I started twitching and became incapacitated. "Stop. It. I. Can't. Breathe," I said between uncontrolled giggles.

He smiled wickedly but didn't stop the torture. "If my muscles are full of air, then why can't you get away? Tell me you were wrong to insult my guns."

I pinched my lips together and shook my head.

"Say it..." he prodded again. This time his fingers moved further up my sides to where I was really, really ticklish. I arched my back and tried to get away, but he didn't budge.

When I still didn't say it, he set his hands on either side of my face and leaned down until his face was only a breath away. "Tell me you were wrong."

My mind went blank before flashing back to yesterday, when he'd put his face this close to mine. Except this time, instead of wanting to turn my head and give him my cheek, I wanted to tip my lips up and capture his with mine.

But that didn't make any sense.

I'd just kissed British Boy this afternoon, how could I suddenly want to kiss Luke, too?

Our eyes caught, and my cheeks burned with heat. Could he tell what I was thinking?

He cleared his throat, his expression sober. "Ok, I'll stop."

A second later he was up and helping me to stand.

"Thanks." I patted my legs and adjusted my shirt so it fell just right over my hips. It took me a moment to gain enough composure to look at him.

"Should we try that lift again?" Luke asked, breaking the awkward silence that had fallen between us.

I nodded my head vigorously. "Yes. Let's do that."

THE NEXT DAY, I decided to push the unsettling feelings I was having for Luke out of my mind and focus on figuring out British Boy's true identity. I wasn't the kind of girl to go around kissing one boy, only to want to kiss another. That wasn't me. So I studied British Boy's hoodie as it sat in the passenger seat of my car on my drive to my early morning drill team practice.

It was a bright red, SUNY Cortland hoodie. When I lifted it to my nose, it smelled like British Boy in the Chemistry lab, which, if I was to be honest, reminded me of what a dad or a grandpa would wear. Not your typical hot-guy-in-a-bottle that I wanted to breathe in all day long. Kind of like Luke's scent at our dance practice yesterday. That was the way a hot guy should smell.

I didn't remember Noah smelling like that either, so unless he'd started wearing a new cologne, it probably wasn't him like I'd initially thought. But I would definitely need to do a little more investigating before I could cross him off my list of suspects.

At lunch period, I set my salad on the table and waited for Eliana to show up. I was hunched over my notepad, trying to figure out some names to add to my suspects' list when Eliana plopped down next to me with her tray steaming with pizza and fries.

"Where's Jess?" I asked. They usually came to lunch together.

She took a bite of a French fry and shrugged. "I saw him walking here with Breanna Murdock. I'm pretty sure he's sitting with her today."

"What? When did that happen?"

"Apparently, that flirting yesterday turned into his next relationship." She stabbed another fry into her ranch, and if I didn't know any better, I'd think she wasn't so happy about my brother dating someone again.

"How long do you think they'll last?"

"I'm betting a week this time." Eliana said.

"Not a fan of Breanna, I guess?" She usually bet at least two weeks.

"Nope. Not a fan."

"Okay, then," I squinted my eyes at her, trying to read why she was reacting this way. Was it possible she was finally starting to realize she and my brother would be perfect together?

Instead of saying anything about it, I said, "I'll give them three days. Winner buys smoothies next time?"

"Deal." After taking a bite of her pizza, Eliana pointed to my notepad. "What's that?"

"It's my list of suspects for British Boy."

"Still only got one?"

I nodded, staring at Noah's name. "I really hope it's not him." I may have confused myself for a moment yesterday, thinking I might have feelings for Luke. But now that my head was clear and I was a safe distance from his intoxicating scent and muscles, I realized that I still wanted to find a way for things to somehow work out between British Boy and me.

And if they were going to work out, British Boy couldn't be Noah. We'd already had our shot. I wanted British Boy to be everything I'd imagined, not someone who had faked everything. He said he'd only faked the accent because he didn't think I'd like him, so if everything else about him was real, I'd be crazy not to forgive him the tiny indiscretion and ask him to trust me with his true self.

"Who else should we add to the list?" I asked Eliana after taking a bite from my salad.

She looked around the cafeteria, so I let my gaze wander the room as well. British Boy was supposedly a senior, so that meant he should be in here if he didn't eat off campus.

Eliana pointed to a table to our right. "What about Kade Isom? He's tall and has dark hair."

I squinted to try and get a better look. "Too skinny." I may have been feeling British Boy through a thick sweatshirt, but I could tell he had a great physique.

I looked around the room some more. My eyes caught on a cute guy sitting at a table in the corner. He had dark brown hair and beautiful caramel-colored skin. "Do you know who that is?" I asked Eliana.

"Who?" She leaned closer to get a better view.

"The guy in the gray and blue striped V-neck." I pointed as discreetly as I could. The guy turned his head and his eyes locked with mine.

My heart stuttered for a second. This guy was hot!

"He's looking at you," Eliana whispered in my ear. "Do you think it's him?"

"I don't know," I whispered back, my blood simmering with anticipation.

Someone stepped into my view, breaking the hot eye contact Suspect Number Two and I were having. When the view cleared again, the guy was walking toward me. And that's all it took for me to look away. He was a shorty. Buff, but way too short to be the guy I'd had to stand on my tiptoes to kiss yesterday.

"Dang." Eliana sighed, noticing the height as well.

I turned back around in my seat, hoping it would give the guy the hint that I wasn't interested after all.

While we waited for the guy to hopefully pass by our table, Eliana took my pen from my hand and scribbled out the words "British Boy" at the top. Then the pen scratched along the white space above it as she wrote the words "Imposter Boy."

I smiled at her. "Brilliant."

I SPENT the next week and a half trying to figure out who Imposter Boy might be, putting names on the list, only to cross them off again after further investigation. I was beginning to wonder if Imposter Boy had lied about the brown hair and brown eye thing, just to confuse me. Because it seemed like I'd found one reason or another to take every guy who fit that description off my list. Every guy except Noah, that is.

The thought that I'd practically thrown myself at Noah in the

Chemistry lab made my stomach turn sour. I hated to think that I might have been kissing the one guy at school that I'd vowed to never kiss again.

But I had to figure out if it was him sooner or later, so instead of looking around at every other guy in the world, I decided to put him to the test. I messaged Imposter Boy a few times since our last meeting but still hadn't received a response. But thanks to the read receipts that awesomemail provided me with, I could tell that he'd been at least reading them...most times almost immediately after I'd sent them.

Which gave me an idea and a safe way to check if it was Noah, without actually having to ask him or sniff him.

So before school on Thursday morning, I positioned myself in the library at a table that had the perfect view of Noah's locker through the window. I waited for him to get there and watched as he pulled out his notebook and turned around to stand with his back against his locker. He looked off into the distance, as if contemplating something very profound. I couldn't ignore the fact that it was exactly something I'd expect Imposter Boy to do. He seemed the deep-thinking kind of guy. Plus, from what Imposter Boy had told me about his dad starting to date someone, I gathered that he came from a broken home. Just like Noah. Coincidentally enough.

Before I could talk myself out of it, I hit send on the message and watched him for a reaction. He didn't move. I held my breath as anticipation bubbled in my throat. Still, he didn't pull out his phone. I didn't know whether to be disappointed or what. Maybe he hadn't felt it vibrate in his pocket? Or maybe he'd left his phone at home?

But when I peeked down at my screen, it showed that the message had been read.

It wasn't Noah.

22

LUKE

I SLIPPED my phone back into my pocket as I walked into school Thursday morning. Ashlyn wasn't making this easy. She wasn't giving up on trying to get British Boy to meet her again. She kept sending me messages about how I didn't need to worry about her finding out who I really was. But that's exactly what I was so freaked out about. How could I not be scared? She'd barely given me a second glance since we started our daily practices, even as we were dancing, our faces a torturous breath away from each other. Anytime I tried to imagine telling her the truth, the only image that came to my mind was of her disappointed face. Disappointed because I wasn't what she was hoping for. I wasn't who she wanted.

But how could she not know that it was me? She was so caught up with the idea of some perfect guy behind the screen that she couldn't see what was right in front of her—right there dancing with her, trying to get her to look at him as more than just a friend or dance partner or old rival. So many times I thought she was feeling something, when we were dancing closely or when I dipped her as the music swelled through the speakers in her family room. She would look straight into my eyes and slowly come toward me. All I wanted to do was pull her closer and let my lips find hers, and whisper that I was the guy she was looking for. But instead of feeling the tiniest bit of romance, she'd step out of my arms, restart the song, and tell me to try the steps again.

All this time I'd assumed that the truth was what was keeping me from her. But holding onto my secret was only making me crazier. I was beginning to wonder if the truth might just be the thing to set me free from this. Even after all my planning, I still didn't have her. So it wasn't like things could get worse. I might as well just tell her that I was British Boy and let the pieces fall where they may.

I walked down the main hall of the school, headed toward my first period class. I was just about to enter my Humanities classroom when an arm linked through mine.

"Good morning, Luke." Ashlyn smiled at me, looking the happiest she'd been in too long.

"You seem cheerful. Something good happen this morning at drill practice?" Her smile made me uneasy. Had she figured out the truth somehow and was just being really sweet before she smacked me?

"Not unless you can call being chewed out by your coach for dancing too sloppily good." She sighed.

"Nope, not my kind of fun. I'm pretty sure I know what you're talking about. Just last week, my dance coach told me my muscles were made of air and that I couldn't dance to save my life."

She slugged me in the arm. "I didn't say that last part."

I smiled. "Fine. So what are you happy about?"

The bright smile was back on her lips. "I just found out the best news."

"Really?" She'd just messaged British Boy a couple minutes

ago. How many other things could she have going on this morning?

She pulled on my arm so we could stop and talk in front of the lockers next to my classroom. "As you may have noticed, I've been a little down lately."

I nodded. "Definitely noticed that."

"Anyway, what I didn't tell you is that I've been worried that my pen pal might have been Noah."

I raised my eyebrows. "Noah?" How in the world did she come to that conclusion?

"Yes, long story. Anyway, I really didn't want him to be Imposter Boy."

"Who's Imposter Boy?"

"Oh." She waved her hand in the air. "That's what Eliana and I decided to call my pen pal after finding out he's been lying this whole time."

I swallowed.

She smiled at me again. "I've been trying to find anyone who fits the little bit of information I have about Imposter Boy, because I was so desperate for him not to be Noah. But after looking at every single guy at school, at least all the seniors, I had no other options left."

Except me, of course. Should I be offended she hadn't even considered me an option? Was I really so far off the radar that she couldn't even give me a second thought? Ouch!

She continued, not seeming to notice that I'd taken offense. "So this morning, I decided I needed to finally bite the bullet and put Noah to the test."

"You told Noah about Bri—about Imposter Boy?" Oops. That was a close one. I wasn't supposed to know that Imposter Boy had once been affectionately named British Boy.

"No, of course not! I didn't even have to talk to him."

"Then how?"

"I messaged him." She shook her head. "Not him, Noah, but him, Imposter Boy. Then I watched to see if he checked his phone."

"And did he?" I asked, playing along now that I had an idea of where she was going with this.

"Didn't even touch it."

"And you don't think he just left his phone at home."

"No, the message was read by the real imposter."

I furrowed my brow in confusion. "How do you know that?"

She looked at me like I was missing something obvious. "It had the read receipt on it." Her face brightened. "So Noah isn't Imposter Boy!"

She said it like it was the happiest thing in the world. Her eyes were sparkling, and she had the biggest smile I hadn't seen her wear in a while.

"I'm glad you figured that out," I said, sincerely.

"Me too."

"So where do you go from here? Still gonna keep trying to solve the mystery?"

She shook her head and adjusted the strap of her bag on her shoulder. "I don't think so. We had some great conversations, and I thought we were really going somewhere. But..." She sighed, her demeanor darkening with sadness. "In the end, he didn't want things to work out. And I know better than to force something that wasn't meant to be."

I nodded, liking the way she was thinking. Maybe my plan had worked after all. She just needed a little more time to move on than I'd thought. But finally, finally, we were officially done with British Boy.

The bell rang. Ashlyn stepped away from the wall. I was turning to walk into my class when she touched my arm. "Oh, I almost forgot. I know I've been working you hard on the dance, but I was wondering if you'd be willing to do one last thing for me on Saturday. There's this club in Syracuse that has an under-eighteen night once a month, and I was hoping we could go and try out our dance moves in a more public setting."

"More public dancing in Syracuse? And will we be wearing our panda heads, too?"

She smiled, and I couldn't help but smile back. "Not this time. And I promise it won't be like a dance practice all night long. We can just do regular club dancing."

I pinched my lips together. "Are we ever going to do anything together that doesn't involve dancing?"

"Once the competition is over with, we can do whatever you want."

"Really?" Warmth flooded my body at those words. She was still planning to hang out after the competition ended. That had to be a good sign.

"Yeah, you can totally teach me how to play football and find a way to embarrass me in front of a crowd of people."

I smiled at the thought of Ashlyn running around the football field in a bunch of football gear.

"Or," she continued. "We could even try watching a movie again sometime. Who knows, maybe it'll turn out differently than last time."

I gulped. Did she just say what I thought she said?

It took me a moment to find my tongue. "I think I might like that."

The second bell rang and the last stragglers hurried into their classrooms.

"I'll see you later, Luke." She stepped backwards as she walked away, looking more beautiful than she ever had before.

I retreated and bumped right into the door. My cheeks burned, and I rubbed the back of my head. "Yeah. See you later."

23

ASHLYN

AFTER DANCING the halftime show at the football game Friday night, I headed back to the bleachers to my spot next to Eliana, Jess, and Breanna. I found Eliana sitting alone on a blanket.

"Where's Jess and Breanna?" I asked Eliana.

Eliana took a sip of her soda before saying, "Breanna got annoyed that Jess was paying more attention to the game than her, so she asked him to take her home."

"You think they're going to break up?"

Eliana shrugged. "It wouldn't surprise me. She was pretty mad."

I rolled my eyes. "*My brother*." When was he going to stop this game? "Oh well, looks like you get to take me out for a smoothie."

Eliana shook her head and laughed. "When will I ever learn?"

The crowd erupted into a huge cheer. I turned my focus to the field below. Number thirty-seven was running toward the goal line with the football tucked under his arm. He darted past one of Solvay High's players, ran across the twenty-yard line, and zigzagged past another player to run across the ten-yard line. The crowd roared louder and the band started playing the celebration song just as Luke crossed over the goal line.

"Go, Luke!" I joined the crowd in cheering. Man, he was good at football. If he played like he was playing tonight, he'd have his pick of colleges offering him scholarships.

Our kicker scored the extra point and kicked off to the other team while Luke grabbed a drink. My heart swelled in my chest when his gaze went to the crowd. I knew there was a fat chance of him actually seeing me, but my heated cheeks didn't seem to understand that.

"Is Luke looking at you?" Eliana whispered.

My heart hammered even more. "You think so?"

She nodded. "I've been watching you guys together the past couple of weeks, and it wouldn't surprise me if he liked you."

"Really?" My throat closed up on me. I couldn't breathe.

"I wasn't going to say anything since you were so occupied with that British Imposter Boy, but I really think he does."

I pinched my lips together, my legs bouncing as I tried to hold Luke's gaze.

"Would you think I'm crazy fickle if I admitted that I might like him too?" I asked when Luke ran back onto the field.

"Not at all," she said. "We can't always decide who we like, or when we finally realize it."

A moment later, Luke was weaving his way through the defensive line. He was so fast and powerful. So incredibly good with the ball. He commanded the whole field when he was out there. It was crazy how much had changed in the past couple of weeks. We were actually really good friends, and now that I'd given up my British Boy addiction, I was finally realizing what had been there all along.

Watching him in his element, you'd never know he was fighting demons of his own. He appeared to be the perfect picture of the All-American high school guy. Popular, friendly, fun, outgoing...and yeah, hot. Really, really hot. If I hadn't seen it with my own eyes, I never would have known he was having such a hard time right now. I wondered how many of his teammates even knew about his mom. It didn't seem like he'd told very many people about her.

"Earth to Ashlyn," Eliana spoke next to my ear, breaking my gaze away from Luke's tall, muscular frame.

I shook my head to get my mind out of the temporary daze. "Sorry. Were you saying something?"

She looked around, as if to assure no one was listening in on our conversation. "Have you ever wondered if Luke might be Imposter Boy?"

My eyes went wide. I felt dizzy at her suggestion. "I—" I licked my lips, which had gone dry at her words. "That never occurred to me."

"He does fit the description. You have to admit that."

I nodded, my gaze back on Luke as he ran off the field for a timeout. Could Luke be the guy I'd been messaging? They were about the same height and build. And the more I'd gotten to know Luke over the past weeks, I'd seen a much different side to him. Him being British Boy would actually be kind of perfect. It would be like having the emotional connection I'd always been looking for, along with the friendship and attraction that I'd always wanted in a boyfriend.

But no. It couldn't be him. I would have known, wouldn't I? They smelled completely different.

"No, I don't think so."

"But it makes you think, doesn't it?"

It did... But, no. It couldn't be him. Luke was known for being a prankster, but there was no way he'd do something like that. He would have said something about it when I talked to him about British Boy. He wasn't the type to lie about something like that.

He was simply just another guy at our school who happened to fit the characteristics for the guy I'd never actually seen.

The whistle blew and the clock started again. We were tied now. Just one more touchdown and we could win.

Jess appeared at the edge of our row. I stood so he could sit on the other side of Eliana.

"Where's Breanna?" Eliana asked him once he'd settled in next to her.

He shrugged and looked out at the field. "We broke up."

"Sorry to hear that," Eliana offered.

He glanced back at her. "It's fine. It was only a couple of weeks. Nothing to cry over."

"Looks like we'll be going out for smoothies after all," I said under my breath to Eliana. She acted like she was annoyed at the thought of losing another bet, but since I was watching carefully, I didn't miss the look of relief in her eyes. She may not know who she liked yet either, but it was obvious she preferred to have my brother sitting beside her. Right where he belonged.

SATURDAY DRAGGED on as I waited for the time for Luke and me to finally hang out. I had the whole evening planned out in my mind. After seeing him at the game and realizing how much I liked him, I couldn't mess things up anymore. I'd already talked way too much about other guys around him, and then I'd been an idiot and turned my head when he tried to kiss me at my house. I didn't have time to waste or room for stupid decisions. So the first thing I needed to do was try to look as good as he did. Which was going to be hard since he looked too good for this earth.

I dug through my closet until I found my favorite blouse—a white, ruffled linen shirt that would go perfectly with my new light pink skirt. I'd noticed Luke eyeing my legs a few times over the past week, so I hoped this would help keep his interest. I went downstairs to wait for him to pick me up.

Eliana and Jess were sitting at the table, playing a game of Boggle when I walked into the dining room. They acted like such an old married couple sometimes.

Eliana raised an eyebrow when she saw me. "What are you all dressed up for?"

"It's not too much, is it?" I smoothed my skirt down with my hands. "Luke and I are going dancing tonight."

Jess turned around to look at me. "Sure, it's fine, if you're into the whole showing-off-your-underwear thing."

Eliana slapped Jess's arm.

"I have shorts under this," I argued.

Eliana turned away from Jess. "Don't listen to your overprotective brother. You look great. Where are you going?"

"Sasha's, that dance club in Syracuse. They're holding an under-eighteen night tonight."

"What a great idea." Jess scooted away from the table. "Eliana and I will join you. Someone has to watch out for you."

I rolled my eyes. "I'm a big girl, Jess. I can handle dancing alone with Luke for one night."

Though maybe this would be a way to finally get them together.

Before I could take back my words, Jess shrugged. "Suit yourself."

Eliana stood next to Jess. "We were about to head to my house anyway. I think my dad was planning to make his famous tiramisu for dessert tonight."

Jess's eyes brightened like she'd just said the magic words. "I do love that."

I mouthed *thank you* to Eliana when my brother's head was turned. She just smiled. She was the best.

They were almost out of the room when Jess glanced back and said, "You can always text us an SOS if Luke starts to get handsy."

Eliana elbowed him in the stomach and he groaned. She looked pointedly at me. "You have a good time. It sounds like we might have a lot to catch up on after tonight."

I nodded and tried to calm my nerves after they left. I hoped I'd have something worth talking to Eliana about after tonight.

A couple of minutes later, the doorbell rang and I hurried to get the door before Mom, Dad, or Macey could embarrass me.

Luke stood on the doorstep in the late-afternoon sunlight, looking drop-dead gorgeous in a dark blue V-neck that did everything for his muscular physique. I swallowed. Maybe Jess should worry about *me* keeping my hands to myself. I'd never been more attracted to someone in my life.

We stared at each other for a moment before I cleared my throat and finally found my tongue. "Uh, ready?" I stepped out of the house and shut the door, suddenly feeling very self-conscious. Luke was on a whole different level of hot than me. What if he didn't think of me as more than just a friend? I'd seen the ultra-thin, popular girls flirt with him plenty at school. What if I wasn't good enough for him?

But his footsteps followed me down the sidewalk, so I tried not to worry too much. He said yes to hanging out with me when he could have said no. He picked me for his dance partner when he could have picked Kelsie or Hannah. Maybe there was a chance that he could like me, too.

24

LUKE

I NEVER THOUGHT Ashlyn could be prettier than she'd been the last time we'd gone to Syracuse and danced with those ridiculous panda heads. But I was wrong. Boy was I wrong. Ashlyn was a goddess. Somehow even more beautiful than she'd ever been. And I got to dance with her tonight.

I may have been scared out of my wits to dance in a public place, without a huge panda mask for protection from onlookers. But if it meant I got to dance with her, I was in. I was so unbelievably in.

As we drove to Syracuse, I kept losing my train of thought because when I looked in her eyes, my mind turned to mush. Almost melted in my head. How was I supposed to form a coherent thought when all my brain could think about was whether I'd finally get to kiss her again tonight? Now that I actually knew what it was like to kiss her, there was absolutely no way I'd be able to stop constantly thinking about it when I was with her.

There was just one problem. I didn't deserve her. I'd thought everything was just fine between us now that she'd decided to give up on finding British Boy. But the guilt was an ever-present thorn in my side. It was almost as strong as my urge to kiss her. Which was pretty dang powerful.

"Have you ever been to a club before?" Ashlyn asked, her expression excited.

I shook my head. "You do recall me telling you I didn't dance before this thing, right?"

She smiled. "Of course. I remember. Sorry, I'm just so excited. I've wanted to do this since forever, but no one would ever go with me."

My chest lightened at the thought that I could make her happy in a way no one else had before. "I'm glad I could go with you, then. But my dancing skills are probably more likely to ruin the night for you than make it better."

She patted my arm, and my skin sparked to life beneath her touch. "You'll do great. You've gotten so much better in just the past couple of weeks. Plus, I seem to remember those *Hitch* moves of yours. You can totally pull those out at the club if that makes you more comfortable."

"I might be able to handle that." I flashed her what I hoped was a dashing smile.

Tell her. My conscience prodded me. *Just tell her the truth. Something like: Hi Ashlyn. You know that guy you call Imposter Boy? That's me. Please don't smack me.*

I shook my head. Yeah, that probably wouldn't turn out like I wanted it to.

She turned on the radio and I was happy for the distraction.

Hey, Ashlyn. Remember that pen pal you fell in love with and were so sad that you couldn't find? It's me. Let's make out.

No.

I studied her out of the corner of my eyes as she stared out the windshield at the oncoming traffic, the lights from the vehicles lighting her face every few seconds.

She looked so happy, peaceful but also excited. I didn't want to ruin that look. If I told her the truth right now, she'd probably insist I take her home and she'd miss out on the dance club experience she'd always wanted. So maybe it would be better for me to just wait and tell her at the end of the night, after she'd had the evening she'd dreamed of.

Just tell her before you kiss her, I told myself. If I waited until later she'd never forgive me. If I told her before then, at least I'd see her hand coming to smack me when she recognized that I kissed the same way as British Boy. If I waited until after the kiss, I'd be blindsided by her fist.

It wasn't long before we pulled into the parking lot behind a building with a huge neon sign that read *Sasha's*. I took a deep breath and shut off the Jeep. So much was riding on tonight. Everything had to go perfectly.

25

ASHLYN

AN UPBEAT TECHNO-DANCE song played as Luke and I walked into the club. The lights were turned down low, and there were couples and singles scattered all over the dance floor. The upbeat music brought me to life, and I immediately wanted to get out there and dance. Dancing was in my blood. I'd been dancing since I was three years old and it was what made me feel alive.

I glanced at Luke to see if he was feeling the music the way I was.

His face had gone pale, and he looked like he wanted to run out the door.

"I can't do this, Ashlyn. Please don't make me go out there and dance in front of all these people." His eyes were full of panic.

I tugged on his arm. "You can do this. You're ready."

When he still didn't budge, I took his hand, a warm sensation slipping up through my arm as I did so, and pulled him through the crowd until we found an open space near the back of the room. It was darker over here, so I hoped Luke would feel more comfortable in the shadows.

"You can just start with your awesome step-touch moves at first. I'll request the DJ to play our song in about an hour." It wouldn't surprise me if his face suddenly turned fluorescent under the black light, because he went even whiter at my mention of our song.

"Do you trust me?" I asked.

"Not exactly," he said, a half smile forming on his lips.

"At least you're honest. I guess I'll never have to worry about you lying to me." I winked.

I'd expected him to laugh at my joke, but he didn't even crack a smile. If anything, he became even more serious. So I decided to take things into my own hands—meaning, taking Luke's hands in mine.

Lights circled around the room in beams of red, blue, green, and purple. I pulled Luke farther onto the dance floor. He stumbled forward as we tried to step to the beat.

"Go easy on me, okay?" he said, his eyebrow raised.

"We'll take things slow. Just one step at a time," I said.

It was like he'd completely forgotten everything we'd worked on the past weeks. His feet were all fumbly again, his movements stiff. And I was so thankful that I'd thought to bring him here tonight instead of discovering his stage fright on the night of the competition.

Eventually, after a few false starts and only a couple of smashed toes, we were dancing—kind of dancing, at least. He was stepping from side to side and I was bouncing to the beat, resisting the urge to spin and leap and create a full-on dance routine.

"It's not so bad, is it?" I spoke loudly to be heard over the music.

"It's okay." Luke glanced self-consciously at the couples surrounding us.

A girl with blue hair sashayed past us, shaking her hips like

Shakira as she danced a circle around her date who was practically drooling over her. There was another couple wrapped so tightly in each other's arms, I wondered how they could breathe, let alone move to the beat. And then there was a pair who'd been making out for the past five minutes. I was tempted to tell them to get a room. Or at least a table in the corner.

It took a few songs, but Luke did loosen up eventually, a glimmer of this past week's work finally shining through.

After I requested our song, we stopped to get drinks. Luke ordered a Dr. Pepper and I did the same.

"You have good taste in drinks." He lifted his glass.

"So do you." I tapped mine against his before taking a sip. "You also have a great choice for dance partners. I never asked you, but what made you choose me anyway? I hadn't exactly been the sweetest before this whole thing started."

He shrugged. "I figured you were the only girl who could handle me. Plus, I saw Noah's name on the list and thought you'd be okay dancing with me if it meant you didn't have to dance with him."

I felt breathless at the thought of him being so considerate. "Thanks for doing that. Things haven't been super awesome between us, so I'd much rather be with you instead of him."

"Just because I'm a better alternative?"

I looked up at his face, and there was something there that made me think his question wasn't as light as he was trying to make it sound.

I cleared my throat. "You *are* a better alternative. But I'd be lying if I didn't admit that I've enjoyed spending more time with you. You're so real and fun, and I know exactly what I'm getting when I'm with you. It's really nice."

My heart pounded so fast after practically telling him that I liked him so much more than I ever could like British Boy.

Instead of running away from me like I was a crazy girl, he

said, "I've enjoyed hanging out with you, too, Ashlyn. You've surprised me."

The piano and cello interlude of *A Thousand Years* started playing over the speakers a few minutes later. I thought I'd told the DJ to wait a while longer, but apparently, now was the moment for us to make our debut.

I turned to Luke, who was already gazing at me with an anxious anticipation in his eyes.

But he didn't hide. Instead, he held his hand out to me. "I guess that's our cue," he said. And there was something different in his voice. It was warmer. Lower. Like he could change one thing about the tone of his voice to push me over the edge of getting lost in him forever.

His gaze captivated me. He gave me a smile that made me want to melt and I couldn't look away. I couldn't get my mouth to form a simple response either. So I took his hand, feeling zaps of electricity at his touch.

Instead of taking me to the back corner where we'd spent most of the evening, he led me to the middle of the dance floor beneath the colorful lights. He put one hand on my back, and the other lifted my hand in his, expertly demonstrating the correct position for our waltz.

Even though I'd been dancing with him all night, somehow this felt different. It was more intimate. There was something in the grip of his hands and the way he pressed against my back that made my insides turn to mush. For the first time, I worried that *I* might actually be the one to forget the steps.

I hesitantly moved closer to him, so our bodies were aligned in the proper closed position. And then we stepped to the music. As we spun around the dance floor, I couldn't help but breathe in Luke's intoxicating cologne. He smelled so good. And for a moment, I broke form and let my head rest against his jaw as we danced. I loved how tall he was. It felt so nice to be held in his strong arms, so close to his body. He seemed calmer than he had been all night, like the romantic music had cast some sort of spell over him. It had definitely bewitched me already.

"How am I doing?" he whispered, his mouth next to my forehead.

"Really good," I admitted. "You're going to wow the judges next weekend."

"It's all because of you." He pulled his head back. When I dared look up at him, I almost burst into flames because his eyes were practically smoldering at me. But why?

Was it the song? Was it the atmosphere? Or was it because of me?

I swallowed, feeling much more nervous than I'd ever felt around him.

He dipped his head closer and said, "I'd try singing, but I'm pretty sure that would ruin the moment."

I laughed, grateful for the humor. "Not a singer?"

"Definitely not."

I smiled. "Me neither."

The music swelled in a crescendo, and Luke spun me out before pulling me back into him for the lift.

I caught hold of his shoulder and let him lift me into the air.

I was weightless as we spun around. I leaned my forehead against his and lost myself as I gazed into his warm, brown eyes.

How did I fail to notice the way he made me feel before? How was it possible that I'd been so caught up in my infatuation with British Boy that I couldn't see this amazing man right before me? I had to be completely blind.

We finished our routine. It was then that I realized we had an audience. The whole room had formed a circle around us and were clapping and cheering.

My cheeks heated as I turned to Luke. He was smiling bashfully at the crowd, but I could see from the look in his eyes that he was proud of himself.

"You did it!" I wrapped my arms around him, the exhilaration from the atmosphere making me shaky.

He folded me into his chest. "*We* did it. You're amazing, Ashlyn."

I hugged him tighter, letting the word *amazing* run through my mind again, committing the way it had sounded into my memory.

"THANKS FOR BRINGING ME HERE," Luke said as we left the club and headed down the sidewalk to where his Jeep was parked.

"Thanks for not bolting when we first got here. I had a lot of fun."

"Me too." We walked in silence, listening to the sounds of the city at night. Cars passed, leaving red taillights for us to follow.

"You're different than I thought," Luke said after a while.

I stopped to look at him, studying his silhouette in the moonlight. "Good different or bad different?"

He returned my gaze, and I felt myself going weak under his stare. "Good different. Very good," he said softly.

We continued down the sidewalk again. I took a chance and slipped my hand into his. I just had to be closer to him again after spending the evening in his arms. He tensed for a moment before letting his fingers curl around mine. Warmth spread throughout my whole body. His hand felt nice in mine, right somehow.

"Is this okay?" I asked, lifting our hands.

"More than okay," he said quietly.

Content, I leaned my head against his shoulder as we walked the last few yards to his vehicle.

He opened the passenger door for me and then climbed in on his side. "Are you ready to go home?" he asked as he stuck his keys in the ignition.

"Not really." But the time on the dash told me it was already eleven o'clock, and if I didn't get home soon I'd be in big trouble. I sighed. "But you better take me home. Even though there are about a million other things I'd rather do than go to sleep right now."

Luke raised an eyebrow. "What kind of things?"

I shrugged, embarrassed, even though I hadn't said anything incriminating yet. "Obviously more dancing. We could totally grab some more panda heads and find a street corner."

Luke shook his head and laughed. "Do you ever stop dancing?"

"Sometimes." I smiled, happy that I'd successfully deflected his question. I wasn't about to admit that I wanted to find a place where we could sit close and see what happened.

Luke pulled out of the parking lot and headed for the highway. He switched on the radio, and soon we had the new Lady Gaga song taking us home. I discreetly studied him as we drove, taking in the shape of him. He sat tall, his shoulders broad, and his lips looked the perfect size and shape for kissing. He was probably a really good kisser, and there was a huge part of me that wanted to find out if my assumptions were true.

"What?" he asked, catching my stare.

My face flushed and I was happy for the darkness. "Nothing."

"Do I have something on my face?" He ran a hand down his cheek to check.

"No. But your profile could rival any Greek god's." I covered my mouth after realizing I'd said my thoughts aloud.

My comment earned a smile from him though, and my cheeks cooled a little.

"A Greek god, you say?"

I laughed awkwardly. "Or perhaps Gonzo? I can't make up my mind."

He shoved my shoulder playfully. "Don't make fun of the nose. Blame it on my Jewish ancestors."

"I actually like your nose. It's so long and dignified."

"Dignified." He sputtered. "Pretty sure that's the first time anyone's ever said that."

"You look nice, Luke."

We parked in front of my house a few minutes later. I didn't want to get out. I didn't want this night to end. Not yet. It had been way too magical. But Luke unbuckled his seatbelt, so I followed suit.

He climbed out and walked to my side of the Jeep, opening the door for me like a true gentleman. I couldn't remember the last time a guy had done that for me...or *if* a guy had ever done that for me.

"You don't have to walk me to the door," I said, not wanting to push my luck. Plus, front-porch goodbyes were always so awkward with unspoken expectations.

Luke offered me his hand to help me down. "I know I don't have to. But I want to."

I didn't let go of his hand as he shut the door behind me. And he didn't let go either.

"I had a really great time tonight, Ashlyn." He leaned against the Jeep instead of walking me up the sidewalk. "Probably one of the best I've had in a long time."

I leaned too so we were facing each other, happy he wasn't in a hurry to say goodbye yet. "Me too." I peered into his dark eyes, made even darker in the moonlight. He was gorgeous.

He ran his thumb along my knuckles, his soft touch sending pulses of electricity up my arm. Could he feel the charge between us? Things were changing so fast.

"Actually," he said, looking at our hands. "The last few weeks have been amazing. I felt so alone after my mom died and I didn't know how to be normal around people anymore. And then you came along and just made everything so much easier. I could finally breathe again."

His gaze met mine, and it may have just been the way the moonlight hit his face right then, but it looked like his eyes were moist around the edges. My heart banged against my ribcage.

Aw, Luke. How could this strong, tortured boy tie my stomach up in knots so?

He blinked, and his jaw worked for a second.

"Sorry," he said, tilting his chin to the side as he wiped the corner of his eye with the heel of his hand. "I just..." He released a deep breath.

What was he trying to say? Was he trying to tell me that he liked me?

Butterflies started dancing around in my stomach at the thought. "Yes?" I asked, breathless with anticipation.

"There's something I—"

He was *so* nervous. It was adorable!

But of course he'd be nervous. I'd totally given him my cheek the last time he tried to show me affection. So I squeezed his hand and decided to help him out. "You don't have to say it, Luke. I know."

His brow furrowed. "Y-you do?"

I nodded. "I figured it out on my own."

"And you're not mad?" He looked so confused.

"Of course I'm not mad. I like you, too."

He gulped. "You do?"

I nodded again. "I'm sorry I've been so blind to what was standing in front of me this whole time. I really don't know why it took me so long to figure it out."

"Don't be sorry." He sighed, and I was so happy. He stepped closer and caressed my cheek with the back of his fingers. Chills erupted all over my skin, followed by a path of fire. "And you're really not mad?" His voice was huskier than usual.

I leaned closer so our lips were almost touching. "Of course not. I—"

I didn't get to finish my sentence because he pressed his lips to mine and kissed me. Gently at first, testing, like he still wasn't sure it was okay. But it was most definitely okay. So I wrapped my arms around his neck and pressed myself closer to him. He reacted by clasping his hands behind my waist and pulling me with him as he leaned back against the Jeep.

We may have danced a lot over the past weeks, but I'd never felt him like this before. His chest was all hard muscle, and I reveled in the feeling of it against me. Unable to resist, I ran my hand along his chest, feeling his heartbeat as it raced away with mine. He was a work of art, and I wished it hadn't taken me so long to find myself in his arms this way.

His hands moved up my back until they were tangled in my hair. His lips were warm and soft, and they lingered as he kissed me slowly, passionately. I couldn't breathe. My heart was beating so fast, it actually hurt. Never before had a first kiss been so easy and effortless. It was like we'd kissed each other before and our lips knew exactly what to do. There was no learning curve or awkward nose bumping. Just an unbelievable fire that left me in a heady daze.

"I've been dying to kiss you like this again," he said against my lips.

But I could barely comprehend his words, my mind had already drifted off. I literally could not think right now. His mouth was taking control of my mind, body, and soul.

26

LUKE

"THIS IS UNBELIEVABLE," Ashlyn whispered against my lips when we broke apart for a second to catch our breath. "Why did we wait so long to do this?"

I had thought the kiss in the Chemistry lab was amazing, but it had nothing on this. Not now that everything was out in the open and I didn't have the guilt creeping in to ruin anything.

I'd never felt so good in my entire life. When she said that she knew I was British Boy, and that she wasn't mad at me, I could have floated into the air. I felt so light. So free. Completely content for the first time since my mom died.

And now I was kissing her. Kissing her like I'd never kissed anyone before.

Her hands knotted in the front of my shirt and she pressed the softness of her body against my chest. She moaned softly, low in her throat, and that was it. I was gone.

And I suddenly knew why people described kissing as melting, because every inch of my body dissolved into hers. My veins throbbed and my heart exploded. I'd never felt like this with anyone before. She moved her hands up my back until her fingers curled in my hair and sent tingles through my body.

I breathed in her light scent—coconut and something else that I'd come to know as just Ashlyn. I wanted to breathe her in forever. I never wanted to stop kissing her.

The space around us evaporated. It was just us next to my Jeep under the big tree in her front yard with the moonlight shining down. No one else existed.

It had only taken a few moments of kissing her and I knew I was addicted for life.

"You can stop eating my sister's face now." A deep voice came from behind us.

We broke apart, and I saw her brother walking down the sidewalk with their friend Eliana.

"Oh my heck, Jess!" Ashlyn said, her eyes wide.

Jess shrugged and continued on his way toward the house next door.

Eliana turned her head over her shoulder and mouthed "sorry" to Ashlyn, and then she quickened her step.

"Sorry about that." Ashlyn's gaze met mine. "My brother can be obnoxiously overprotective sometimes."

I ran a shaky hand through my hair. "Don't worry about it. I needed to get my wits about me, anyway."

She sucked in a deep breath and released it slowly. "Me too."

There was so much life sparking in her eyes, and I wanted to kiss her again. But we just stood there, staring at each other for a while, so much being said without words.

Finally, she bit her lip and sighed. "I better go."

I nodded. "Yeah, me too."

But neither of us moved.

Jess was back again, but without Eliana this time. "You guys just gonna stare at each other all night?"

Ashlyn groaned and rolled her eyes. "I'm gonna go now."

I shoved my hands in my pockets. "Okay."

She stepped backward slowly, still not looking away from me. "See you at school on Monday?"

I nodded, and on a whim decided to bring back my British accent for fun, since I knew how much she loved it. "I'll be waiting with bated breath."

She stilled, her smile immediately gone. Had that line really been that stupid?

"What did you just say?" she asked.

So I said it again.

"You're—" She stepped back, as if shocked for some reason. "You're British Boy?"

27

ASHLYN

I STARED AT LUKE, my lips starting to tremble. I wanted to get those words—that accent—out of my head. I was hearing him wrong. This was not real. The sidewalk was not falling out from under me.

Luke couldn't be British Boy.

His brow furrowed. "I thought you said...? Didn't you just tell me that you knew and that it was okay?"

I shook my head vehemently. "No. I didn't say that at all. I thought you were trying to tell me that you liked me. Not that you've been lying to me for weeks."

I was going to throw up. Everything between us had been fake? Was this his idea of the ultimate prank to end the pranking war he'd started so long ago? I could only imagine the lengths he must have gone through in order to pull this off.

He'd known who I was from the very first day in the Chemistry lab and had lied to me right from the start. He manipulated me into falling in love with a fake guy. And as if that wasn't enough, he just had to deliver a bigger blow by making me like him.

I swallowed back the tears threatening to spill. There was no way I was going to cry now. He made me look like a fool. How he even managed all of it, I didn't know. What was his endgame in this whole thing?

To hurt me? Did he hate me that much?

I clutched my stomach, my fingers curling into fists. I was indeed a fool and he played me well.

Luke stepped closer to me. He looked scared. Like he was worried I might go rabid dog on him. But that could all have just been an act too, like everything else he'd done to me.

"I can explain everything."

"So you can lie to me some more?" I snapped at him, holding my hands out to stop his approach. "You took my trust and threw it in the trash. I told you things that I've never told anyone before. What did you plan on doing with that information? Were you planning to post it all over the school once you've compiled your list? Or were you going to wait until the dance competition where you could humiliate me on the big stage in front of the crowd?"

"I wouldn't do that to you."

Wow, he was really good at this. He sounded so sincere that my heart almost believed him.

"You pretended to be a British Boy who suffered from panic attacks. A guy who was all alone in a new country. I felt bad for you, Luke. You played into my compassion in the very worst way. Did your mom even really have cancer? Or was that just another lie?"

He flinched and stumbled back like I'd punched him in the gut.

Well, good. It was his turn to be hurt.

"I trusted you, Luke." My voice came out low and strangled, and I knew I had to end this conversation before I started crying. "How could you play me like that? It was all real to me."

"It was real to me, too," he said, his jaw flexing. "All of it."

My body felt heavy, completely drained from all the emotions I'd felt tonight. "I don't know what to believe anymore, Luke. I literally can't trust my senses around you."

Luke stepped forward again, holding his hands out. "If you would just let me talk to you, you'd understand."

I shook my head, too exhausted to listen to his lies. "I can't talk to you. I can't listen to you. I can't be around you."

"I tried to tell you, Ashlyn. So many times I tried to tell you who I was. But you never even considered me an option when you were trying to figure it out."

"Oh, I considered it. For a second. But I never pursued it because I didn't think you could stoop so low." I drew in a shaky breath. "Just tell Max that we can't do the competition after all. Claim irreconcilable differences or something like that."

I turned and stomped my way to the door, my heels clacking on the sidewalk.

"Ashlyn, wait! Don't do this!" he called after me.

I gripped the doorknob then turned back to him. "You should have just let me dance with Noah."

I ONLY MADE it halfway up the stairs before my eyes were blurry with tears.

Why did things like this always have to happen to me? Was I ever going to be more than just a girl to mess around with? Was any guy ever going to be able to take me seriously?

I shut myself in my room and fell across my bed as the tears trickled out the sides of my eyes.

Maybe I needed to just stop trying to date in high school. I wasn't cut out for it after all. Maybe I had some sort of Brooks family curse. Jess and I certainly sucked when it came to finding love.

I reached for my stuffed teddy wedged between my pillows. Mr. Bear had been my source of comfort as a toddler, and right now, I needed him too. His big brown eyes looked at me with pity—

Brown eyes, just like Luke's.

A sob hitched in my throat. How could he do this to me? I thought he was everything I'd ever wanted in a guy. He made me laugh and he knew how to make me feel better on bad days.

And that smile—I clasped my hand over my heart, to try to stop it from tearing apart inside my chest—his smile had been one of my favorite things.

I buried my face in Mr. Bear's soft tummy. Was any of it even real? The laughter, the fun...his kiss?

I curled up into a ball. Luke betrayed me, my trust. All those times I told him about British Boy and it was him all along. Did he mock me behind my back?

My phone vibrated beside me. Probably Eliana wanting me to dish about tonight.

Luke: **Please don't shut me out. It was all so real. That's why I stopped British Boy when I did.**

My head pounded. I wanted to believe him. I really did. But it was just too much. There had been way too many lies between us.

I deleted his message, as well as all the other texts he'd sent me. Then I went to my awesomemail chat app and scrolled through the messages British Boy had sent me. All these conversations had meant so much. I'd thought I'd finally found someone who got me. But they were all lies. He didn't understand me. And now he never would.

With a few taps on my screen all our conversations were gone.

28

LUKE

I WAITED outside Ashlyn's house for hours, hoping she'd let me come in. But when she didn't respond to my messages, or answer my calls, I drove around until the gas light came on.

How could a night that had gone so amazingly well turn out to be one of the worst nights of my life? I'd thought I'd finally done it. Finally achieved what I'd been hoping for. Finally found the happiness that had been missing since my mom died. But it was all a mirage. Always right in front of me but never within my reach.

I stumbled into my house hours later and found my dad sitting alone in the living room, watching TV. I'd successfully avoided him since that fateful dinner, and I wasn't about to change that now. I didn't need anything else to add onto the crap pile that was my life. So I closed the door as quietly as I could and tiptoed through the kitchen.

His voice cut through the air. "Come and sit down with me, Luke. We need to talk about Amy." He flicked the TV off with the remote.

Talking to him about that new lady friend of his was about

the last thing I needed right now. My blood boiled just thinking that he could move on from my mom after only a few months. Had he even loved her at all?

I'd only been friends with Ashlyn for a couple of weeks and I already knew I'd never get over her even if she never forgave me.

I was at the edge of the stairs that led to my bedroom. Maybe I could pretend I hadn't heard him.

"I know you heard me," his voice called.

I hung my head and sighed before turning on my heel and slinking into the room. I dropped into the chair across from him.

My dad cleared his throat. "I wanted to apologize to you about what happened a couple of weeks ago. That was a terrible way to tell you about Amy."

I cringed at her name.

"I know that must've been a shock. And I'm sorry about that. I just hope you know that nothing was happening between us, between me and Amy, when your mom was still alive. We were just friends at that time." He ran a hand through his hair, which was more silver than brown these days. "But then, I don't know, it was nice to have someone to talk to. You must understand how something like that could happen."

I crossed my arms. "Maybe you should've talked to me instead, Dad. You left me alone after Mom died. Do you know how horrible that felt? It was like losing Mom and you at the same time."

His expression fell. "I'm sorry about that, Luke. I had no idea you felt that way. You should've told me."

I scoffed. "You wanted me to call you on the phone at your work and tell you I was having a panic attack?"

My dad's eyes etched with concern. "You're having panic attacks?"

"Why do you think I ran out of here when you told me? I was having a major freak out."

He looked down. "Do you want me to take you to see a therapist or something? I thought the school counselor was helping with that. Is that not enough?"

"You don't get it, Dad!" I threw my hands in the air. "I don't want to talk to some stranger about my feelings. I want to talk to someone who actually gives a crap about me. I want to talk to someone who knew Mom!"

He flinched at my words. "I'm..." He looked like he had no idea what to say to me. Like I was some strange messed-up kid that he didn't know the first thing to do with.

"You know what?" Tears pricked at my eyes. "I'm doing fine, Dad. You don't have to worry about me." I stood from the chair and headed toward the stairs. "You can just go on and date whoever you want. I'll remember Mom for the both of us."

He could start his new family and I could just be alone. I was getting pretty good at that.

29

ASHLYN

I SPENT most of the next day in my room, watching movies and pigging out on junk food, trying not to think about Luke. I hated myself for being such a cliché, but Netflix and ice cream were a cliché for a reason. I had to find a way to numb myself from all thoughts of Luke and how it would be to see him tomorrow at school. I needed to make sure that I was indifferent and that the thought of never kissing him again didn't have any sort of effect on me.

I took a break from my mindless TV binging around four o'clock, so I could finish up my Math homework. But once that was done it was back to watching movies.

Of course I couldn't watch any of my old favorites. My BBC collection would forever be ruined for me. Anytime I heard a British accent from now on would remind me of how badly I'd been lied to by Luke. So I turned on *Stranger Things* and hoped it would scare me enough that I wouldn't be able to think about Luke and his brown eyes or the way he'd kissed me before everything fell apart.

TAP TAP TAP.

I awakened with a jolt. Was it a tree branch blowing in the wind and hitting my window? I held my breath and listened some more.

Tap tap tap.

My heart thundered in my ears and I pulled my covers over my head. It sounded too rhythmic and deliberate to be a tree.

Tap tap tap.

Someone was at my window. My two-story window...

"Ashlyn." I heard my name, soft and faint. Like it was being whispered.

My serial killer knew my name.

"*Ashlyn.*" Whoever was outside my window spoke louder and clearer. This time I could tell that it was a man's voice.

I turned on my side and pulled my legs toward me so I was curled up in a ball. Watching *Stranger Things* really hadn't been the best idea after all.

"Open up, Ashlyn. It's just me."

The voice sounded familiar. Had Luke come to apologize some more? Did I want to let him?

I pushed the covers back on my bed, just to go see what he wanted. He had climbed all the way up a tree outside my window. I didn't want him to slip and fall. So I turned on my lamp to see what was going on. I stood by my window for a moment, trying to calm my erratic heartbeat, my heart telling me there was still a chance of it being a murderer outside my window and not Luke. After drawing in a deep breath, I opened my blinds.

I about jumped out of my skin. There was indeed a tall figure right in front of my window wearing a dark hoodie. And it didn't look like Luke. I jerked the blinds shut again.

Why did I open the blinds? What a stupid thing to do. Now my murderer knew I was in my room.

"I know you saw me, Ashlyn. Please let me in."

"Luke?" I asked. He didn't sound exactly like Luke, but my brain was too foggy to think of who else it might be.

"It's me, Noah. Can you please open the window?"

My heart stopped thundering in my chest. It was just Noah.

I unlocked my bedroom window and let him in. "What are you doing here?" I whispered as he stumbled into my room.

I gasped when I saw his face. His eye was swollen shut and he had blood dripping from a gash on his brow.

"What happened? Are you okay?"

He staggered the rest of the way in and sat down on a chair. "I got in a fight with my stepdad."

My throat constricted. "He did this to you?"

"Yeah. It's not the first time either." Noah touched the spot on his head, his fingers coming away bloody.

Worried he was going to get blood on my carpet, I pushed him into my bathroom. "Here," I said, giving him my hand towel. "Put this on your head. I'll be right back with an ice pack." I slipped out of my room as quietly as I could, stepping softly so I wouldn't wake anyone. If my parents discovered I had a guy in my room, my ex-boyfriend nonetheless, they'd kill me.

But then again, if they saw his face maybe they'd think I was beating him up for being there. Still, I'd rather not get caught and have to explain everything.

So, I tiptoed down the stairs, careful to avoid the one that always creaked, and sped my way through the kitchen. I filled a Ziplock bag with ice cubes then carefully retrieved the first-aid kit and a washcloth from the main bathroom just down the hall from my parents' bedroom. My mom was a super light sleeper, so this was the real test.

The door creaked as I shut it.

Crap!

More worried about getting caught than being careful anymore, I rushed down the hall, past the kitchen, taking the stairs two at a time before finally slipping into my room. I shut the door behind me and leaned against it as I tried to catch my breath. If my parents let me have a lock on my door, I would have locked it, too.

When I turned around, I found Noah lying along the foot of my bed with the towel still pushed to his forehead, his legs hanging off the edge.

"Is it still bleeding?" I asked, moving toward him.

"Maybe," he said in his gravelly voice.

"Here, let me look." I reached over and slowly inched the towel away from his cut. When no new blood appeared after a few seconds, I decided he was okay enough to be bandaged up.

I opened the first-aid kit and dug through it until I found the kind of bandage that helped hold gashes together.

"I'm not sure if you'll need stitches or not, but hopefully this will help you avoid getting too big of a scar," I said as I stuck it on his eyebrow.

When our gazes met, he studied me quietly with the eye that wasn't swollen. "Thanks, Ashlyn. I really appreciate it. I didn't have anywhere else to go."

I nodded, smoothing my hand over the skin just above the cut. "It's okay." I sighed. "I wish you didn't have to deal with this."

"Yeah. I wish my mom would stop going back. He's a total douchebag."

"Does he hurt her, too?" I wrapped the washcloth around the icepack and gently set it over Noah's bruised eye.

"He tried. Hence my black eye." He took over holding the icepack to his head, and I busied myself with putting away the first-aid kit.

I looked at the time on my phone. It was after two in the

morning and I had to wake up in just over three hours for drill practice.

"I know it's late, and you're probably tired," Noah said when he noticed me checking the time. "And I know I have no right to ask this of you, let alone even be here right now after everything I've done. But can I just stay here? I promise I'll leave first thing in the morning."

"I don't think having you spend the night here would be a good idea," I said carefully, watching him for a reaction.

Noah swallowed, and I saw fear in his face. "My mom and sister went to the women's shelter. I can't go back home alone tonight. If I do, I'll kill him."

"Noah..." My heart broke for this boy who I used to love. "You're eighteen now. If you let your temper get the better of you, you'll go to jail."

"I know." He closed his eyes and blew out a long breath. "I just...I need to get my mom and sister out of there for good. I'm just so tired right now." He looked exhausted, like he'd been awake for a thousand days. I brushed his hair out of his eyes. It was longer than it had been the last time I'd touched it but still just as soft.

I kissed his forehead, my heart squeezing in my chest for this man who was still a boy. "Okay. You can stay. But you're leaving first thing in the morning."

"Thanks, Ashlyn," he said, sounding like he was already drifting off to sleep. "Luke's a lucky guy. I wish I'd been good enough to keep you forever."

My eyes stung with tears as I dropped a blanket over Noah before curling up in my chair in the corner with a blanket and pillow. I turned on my side and wiped away a tear that slipped out, thinking about how I seemed destined to always fall for guys who never realized what I was until it was too late.

30

LUKE

THE NEXT MORNING, I woke up at five-thirty so I'd have time to run to Walmart—the only store in Ridgewater open at this hour—and buy Ashlyn a bouquet of pink flowers. They weren't the perfect floral arrangement from a florist, but they would have to do for today.

I'd given her some space yesterday, hoping she'd have time to think things through and realize that what I'd done wasn't as bad as she'd thought. But today was a new day, and I'd be seeing her at school, so I wanted to clear the air before it became a big public show.

Flowers in tow, I drove to Ashlyn's house and parked in her driveway, right behind the garage I'd seen her park her Mercedes in before.

At six-fifteen, the garage door opened and revealed her with her drill team bag slung over her arm, her hair pulled up in a high ponytail. She opened the back door and threw her bag in, not seeming to notice me or my vehicle.

I jumped out of the Jeep with flowers in hand. *Here goes nothing.*

I cleared my throat. "Ashlyn."

She jumped and clasped a hand to her chest. "You startled me."

I stepped closer and held out the flowers. "Sorry to scare you. I need to talk to you."

Her expression, which had been surprised for a second, turned hard. "I don't have time to talk to you, Luke. I have to get to practice." She didn't even move to take the flowers from me.

Feeling dumb, I let my hand drop to my side. "I'll drive you then. We can talk on the way," I said, desperate.

"I don't have the energy for this right now. Get in your car and let me leave." She sounded so tired and defeated. I really had broken everything.

"Won't you at least let me explain? Please?"

"So you can lie to me some more?" She shook her head and opened her car door. "I really have to get to practice, Luke. I can't talk to you right now."

The door that led into her house from the garage opened again and out shuffled a tall figure in a dark hoodie who lifted his head at us. I'd expected to see Jess's face peeking up from beneath the hood; instead, Noah narrowed his eyes at me.

My legs threatened to buckle and I had to grip onto the Jeep for support. What was he doing here?

Did he and Ashlyn...? I swallowed. No. She wouldn't go back to him, would she?

They both climbed into her car though, apparently not wanting to give me any answers.

I got into the Jeep and started it with a shaky hand. I backed out of the Brooks' long driveway and pulled along the curb to try and regain control of my senses. Ashlyn's black Mercedes backed out of the driveway, her tires rolling right over the flowers I'd dropped in my shocked state.

She might as well roll over my heart while she was at it.

I FOUND Max Knowles as soon as I got to school. "Can I talk to you for a sec?" I asked him.

"Sure, Luke." He pushed his glasses farther up his nose.

I cleared my throat. "Okay, I just needed to let you know that Ashlyn and I have to drop out of the competition."

"You can't do that," he said very matter-of-factly with a quick shake of the head.

"What do you mean we can't do that?" I asked, confused at such a fast response.

He clasped his hands together. "We already had two couples drop out: Piper Bass broke her ankle last week and Lincoln Dangerfield got a doctor's note saying he can't compete."

"But—" I licked my lips. I hadn't expected Max to put up a fuss about this. "—Ashlyn and I can't work together."

"You picked her in the beginning, knowing full well what you were getting into." Max crossed his arms. "I questioned you from the start, asking if you really thought you could work together, given your past, and you assured me, against my better judgement, that this partnership would work. So I'm sorry to be a tough guy on you, Luke, but you're just gonna have to stick with it."

I shook my head. "No, but you don't understand. This has nothing to do with—"

He held up his hand to silence me. "Nope. Just stop right there. I already have too much drama going on in putting this thing together. It's time for you two to suck it up and make it work. I'll see you at the competition." And before I could say anything else, he walked away.

I FINALLY TRACKED Ashlyn down during lunch. She was sitting at her usual table with Eliana and Jess.

"Hey, Ashlyn." I cleared my throat and decided to get this over with as quickly as possible. She turned to face me, a flash of irritation in her eyes.

She crossed her arms. "What?" Okay, she was even more annoyed with me than she'd been this morning.

"We can't drop out of the competition."

Her eyes narrowed. "What do you mean we can't drop out of the competition? Did you even talk to Max about this?"

"Yes, of course." I held my hands out in front of me as if they could shield me from her irritation. "I don't want to do this any more than you do. But Max says we can't quit."

Ashlyn crossed her arms. "Did you tell him *why* we can't do it?"

"I tried, but he didn't care." I sighed and shrugged my shoulders. "He says we just have to work it out. I guess he figures that we weren't that great of friends when we first started so it shouldn't be much different now."

Ashlyn rolled her eyes. "Oh, things are way different than they were before that. Back then, I thought you were just my nemesis. I had no idea the lengths you would go to just to pull off a prank."

I hated that she still thought everything had been a big joke to me. But I also hated what I'd seen this morning.

"And how is Noah doing these days? I can't believe you'd take him back after everything you told me."

"You mean, everything I told British Boy."

I rolled my eyes. "Whatever."

Arguing with her wouldn't help anything.

But it still boggled my mind that she could go back to him, a guy who had made her miserable for months. How could she take him back after everything he'd done, and not even give me a chance because I pretended I was from England. That was the only lie I'd told her. But apparently, that lie was the only thing she'd liked about British Boy in the first place. Everything else she was left with, everything else that was the real Luke Davenport, wasn't good enough for Ashlyn Brooks. When she had all the parts of Luke lined up together, it just wasn't what she wanted.

I scrubbed a hand through my hair. "I'm willing to stick this thing out, but if you really can't stand the idea of spending one more moment alone with me, go ahead and talk to Max. Maybe he'll listen to you better."

I DIDN'T HAVE to wait long before I found out the result of Ashlyn's conversation with Max. She sent me a text during the next period.

Ashlyn: **Talked to Max. I guess we're stuck, but I will be making some changes.**

What kind of changes? I didn't have a good feeling about this.

Ashlyn: **I'll come by around seven tonight. Be ready to learn fast.**

THE REST of the day rambled on. Football practice was actually okay today. Noah didn't seem as determined to flatten me as much as usual. He did have a black eye and a pretty big cut on his face like he'd already gotten his aggression out on someone earlier. But maybe he was just being nicer because he'd already won the battle we'd never officially announced we were having. The battle for Ashlyn.

Ashlyn came to my house around seven, just as I was finishing up my homework. I ran down the stairs and let her in.

"Hey, Luke," she said, her voice holding just the right amount of iciness to bring my guard right up.

"Hey," I said, not liking her mood. She was not going to be patient with me today.

As if reading my thoughts, she walked in and said, "Let's just get this practice over with, okay?"

She went to the stereo and connected her phone to the speakers before turning back to me. "I've been thinking about our dance all afternoon and I've come up with the perfect way to make this partnership still work. We're going to go in a completely different direction."

"But we have less than a week. We can't start a new dance now."

She raised an eyebrow, challenging me. "I guess you should have thought about that before you decided to pull your stupid stunt." Then her expression changed, suddenly turning sweet. Too sweet. "But don't worry, I found the perfect song. And the choreography is going to be awesome. I think the crowd will love it."

She pressed a button, and the fast, upbeat music of Beyoncé's *Single Ladies* started playing.

My stomach filled with dread. She wouldn't have picked the most humiliating song for a guy to dance to for nothing. She wanted revenge.

"Are you sure about this?" I asked, carefully.

"Yep." She crossed her arms, daring me to challenge her. "I'm in charge, so don't question my judgement. Okay?" she snapped.

"Wow, someone woke up on the wrong side of the bed."

She glared at me and forced any other retort I had back in my throat.

I wanted her to tell me something about last night, preferably that she had slept alone in her bed. But she just turned her back to me and tightened the elastic around her hair.

I stepped closer. "You did sleep last night...?" I let the question hang in the air.

"I don't think that's any of your business now, is it." She turned back toward me, her eyes looking slightly moist. "Now if you're done wasting my time, I'd appreciate it if you'd join me."

I pushed the coffee table out of the way and stood beside her. She paused the music. "You've seen the music video for this right?"

I swallowed. "Hasn't everyone?"

"Just wanted to make sure." She faced the entertainment center. "Stand behind me and do exactly what I do."

I did as she said, not daring to risk the wrath of Ashlyn even for a second.

"We're going to first close our legs to open for the prep," she said while doing what I assumed must have been the move she'd just described. "Prep, prep, open up to the right. One, two, stop and point at your ring finger. Then you're going to go down toward your left, move your booty around, and bring it back up. Hit your head to your hand, and then bring it back up."

Whaaaaat?

"Now it's your turn." She looked at me expectantly.

I stood frozen in my spot, having no idea what she'd just done.

"Come on, Luke. Show me." She cocked her eyebrow and started the song over again. "And five, six, seven, eight." She clapped.

I crossed my arms and shook my head. "I'm not doing that. And even if I was, I don't know the first thing you told me to do."

"Then fake it. You're pretty good at that." She spat the words at me.

The front door opened, and my dad stepped in.

"Hey, Luke," he said. Dad smiled, shutting the door behind him and setting his golf clubs in the closet. "And who's this?" He looked at Ashlyn.

"This is Ashlyn, Dad. Ashlyn, this is my dad."

She wiped at her eye and forced a smile. "Nice to meet you, Mr. Davenport."

"Did I interrupt something?" My dad looked between us.

"No. We were just practicing that dance I told you about. But I seem to be frustrating Ashlyn with my clunky feet."

He grinned. "We Davenport men aren't known for our dancing skills. Nora always begged me to take her dancing when we were younger." He glanced briefly to me, his eyes holding a hint of sorrow at the mention of Mom. "I hated every minute of it back then. Never felt so out of place in my life. But I'd give anything to do it again."

I watched Ashlyn to see if she was going to tell my dad what kind of a son I'd turned into since my mom died. But instead of looking like she wanted to smack me with her fancy purse, she seemed sorry for me. Like she wondered what kind of loser pretended to be someone else just so he had someone to tell his sob story to.

After an awkward silence, my dad clapped his hands together. "Anyway, don't mind me. I'll let you get back to your practice now." He went into the kitchen.

Ashlyn unhooked her phone from the stereo. "I don't think I'm going to be able to practice today, after all. Just work on the waltz on your own this week. We'll run through it a few times on Saturday morning before the competition and call it good."

I nodded, surprised she was still willing to give it a try even then. "I'll do that."

"Oh, I almost forgot." She dug into her oversized purse and

pulled out something red. "Here's your hoodie back. I just love how you went so far as to make it smell like an old man. Nice touch." She threw my dad's Cortland State hoodie at me before walking out the door.

31

ASHLYN

THE NEXT FEW days were long and hard. I tried my best to keep Luke off my mind. Tried to avoid seeing him at all costs, going as far as taking different routes to my classes so I wouldn't risk walking past him. But I couldn't avoid him everywhere. He was there in the lunchroom, sitting at his usual table with his friends, making them all laugh with his latest joke. He was at the pep assembly, participating in the skit because he was one of the stars of the football team. He was in the parking lot, grabbing his duffel bag for football practice, watching me with his brooding eyes as I drove past him. And he was there every night in my dreams, haunting me with thoughts of what might have been if everything hadn't been a lie.

"Do you have to practice with Luke tomorrow?" Eliana asked as I did my makeup for my drill team performance at the game that night.

I set my eyeshadow brush in its cup on my vanity. "Yeah. It's going to be torture."

"You miss him though, don't you?" It wasn't a question, really, because it was obvious to anyone who paid attention to me.

I let my eyes meet hers through the mirror. "I shouldn't, but I do."

"Because he was British Boy?"

I sighed, my heart throbbing in my chest to remind me it was in there, still broken. "Because he was *everything*. I fell in love with both sides of him. He was... He was all the things I never knew I wanted. All the things I never thought I'd have."

Eliana gave me a sad smile. "Then why don't you talk to him? Forgive him."

"I want to. But every time I think I know what to say to him, I remember the look in his eyes when he saw Noah at my house. And the fact that he could even think that I'd thrown myself right back into Noah's arms makes me think he didn't even know me at all."

"So tell him the truth."

I twisted in my chair to face where she sat on my bed. "But what if I tell him and he doesn't want me? What if it really was all a big joke to him?"

"Then you'll be no worse off than you already are, right?"

I turned back to the mirror, hating how practical she was. "It's so easy for you to say that."

She smiled. "I know. I'm like the biggest hypocrite since I've never even gotten close to dating anyone. But I hate seeing you so depressed."

Finished with my makeup application, I stood and grabbed my drill bag from the floor. "I'll see what I can do. Let me just get through tonight first."

I DROVE to the school an hour before the game so I could warm up with the drill team and go through the dance a few more times before tonight's half-time show. We'd be performing our hip-hop number for the first time tonight, and I was excited for my tumbling pass at the end. My back handsprings had been off all week, so I hoped I could pull it together before I splatted on my face in front of the whole school.

We were going through our mandatory stretching routine when Noah walked into the gym and motioned for me to come talk to him. Coach wasn't in the room, so I went to him, trying not to feel a sense of *déjà vu* from all the times we'd talked before games last year.

He took me back to our usual corner by the stairs that let up from the gym.

"Did your mom find you a place yet?" I asked him in a low voice. We had talked a few times this week. Last he'd told me was that his mom was still staying at the shelter and trying to find an apartment for him and his sister to move into. He wasn't telling me where he was staying, which had me wondering if he was sleeping in their car. I really hoped not.

He shook his head. "No, she decided not to press charges."

"She what?" My voice raised an octave, coming out louder than I'd planned. I glanced around to see if Coach had come back. After assuring that I wasn't in trouble, I spoke in a lower voice. "Again?"

He nodded. "I don't understand it. She says I can move in with my dad if I don't like it."

"Which isn't much better."

"I know." He rolled his eyes and bounced his football bag up higher on his shoulder. "Anyway, I've been meaning to thank you for Sunday night."

I looked up just in time to see Luke a few feet away, dressed in his football gear, holding his helmet in his hand.

He walked past us, his shoulder not so gently bumping against Noah as he did so.

"Hey, watch it." Noah growled after him.

"Sorry, didn't see you there," Luke called back before jogging up the stairs.

"Does he not know that I invited myself over Sunday night and that you slept in a chair?"

I shrugged, watching Luke's retreating back. "Probably. I don't need to justify anything to him."

"Hey," he said, making me meet his eyes. "I can tell him the truth if you want. I've already caused enough problems in your life. I don't want to ruin things between you two."

I shook my head. "It's fine. We were having problems before you came over."

"Sorry to hear that."

"Don't be. We were pretty much doomed from the start. I just didn't know it."

"Are you sure you don't want me to talk some sense into him?" he offered.

"No, if he really wants to fix things, he'll talk to me."

"If you say so." He checked the time on his watch. "I better get changed. Good luck dancing tonight."

I nodded. "Thanks. Good luck on your game."

OUR OLD RIVALS, the Westview Tigers, were proving to be worthy opponents tonight. Their players were huge and fast. Each time we got inside the twenty-yard line, they'd stop us from scoring or we'd turn the ball over. I'd never been a huge fan of football in the past, but this game was intense. When half-time rolled around, the score was tied, seven to seven.

The crowd cheered for the drill team as we walked out, ready to do our Hip Hop Mashup. I tightened my black-and-red plaid shirt around my waist as we waited for the announcer to call us to the field.

"Please welcome the Ridgewater High Drill Team," the announcer's voice boomed through the speakers. "Let's make some noise!"

We hit our first formation and the crowd cheered. The music came over the speakers a moment later—a loud, upbeat song with a grungy feel. The noise level went up even louder as we popped and locked to the beat. Hip hop was one of my favorite dances—so strong and empowering—and it was a huge crowd pleaser.

My heart pounded; it was almost time for my tumbling pass. The grass was damp with rain from earlier this afternoon, so I hoped I wouldn't slip and ruin the moment. The music cut and changed, which was my cue to get ready. Just eight more counts until my teammates would part the center for me. I stood on my mark, drew in a deep breath, rolled my shoulders back, and ran forward. My hands hit the grass hard as I did a round off, back handspring, back tuck, the world blurring and spinning as I did it. I stuck my landing and the crowd cheered—a loud roar that coursed over me. A huge grin stretched across my face. This was why I loved dance. The thrill, the anticipation, and then the payoff.

Energized, I found my way back to my spot and finished the routine with my teammates. We were so in sync tonight, the energy between us like something I'd never found anywhere else. Our hive intelligence bonded us together like sisters as we danced on the field.

The music came to an end and we struck our final pose. Kelsie counted out for us to get in line, and then we marched off the center of the field to watch the cheerleaders lead everyone in the school song. I found a spot to sit in the front, surrounded by my teammates, breathing hard and exhilarated from the three-minute performance.

The cheerleaders started the school chant, "W-W-W-O-L-L-

L-V-E-R-I-I-N-N-E-S-WOLVERINES." And a moment later, the pep band began playing the familiar fight song.

Out of the corner of my eye, I noticed the football players lining up just outside the gate. Leading the team was number thirty-seven: Luke. He had his helmet on, so I couldn't really tell, but it almost appeared like he was looking in my direction. My heart pounded as I glanced around. When I checked behind me, I saw his dad down the sidewalk, wearing the hoodie I'd given Luke back on Monday, holding the hand of a red-headed woman in a blue-and-white Ridgewater High sweatshirt.

For a moment I imagined it must be his mom, but a split second later, I realized that it had to be the girlfriend British Boy had messaged me about. I swallowed and turned my gaze back to where Luke was. He shook his head briefly, as if trying to get that image out of his mind. He bounced in place, and as soon as the cheerleaders had cleared off the field, he was running, leading the team out to warm up again.

32

LUKE

HOW COULD my dad show up with her—that woman—after not coming to any of my other games this year? Why had he chosen tonight? One of our biggest games? And with her?

Our game against Westview had always been my mom's favorite game of the year. She was a Ridgewater High Alumni and loved to see us beat her old rival just as much as I enjoyed beating them.

Why did my dad think tonight was the night to finally act like a parent? I wanted to hit something. I wanted to punch him. But since he was safely sitting in the stands, one of Westview High's players would have to do. The guy in front of me better watch out because I was about to take out my frustrations on him.

33

ASHLYN

SOMETHING WAS GOING on with Luke tonight. His game was off, and he looked like he was begging to get pulled out. I wondered if his dad showing up with that woman was the reason behind it. But he needed to get his head back in the game, because if he continued to play like he had been, Coach Hobbs was sure to bench him.

Westview's fullback, number twelve, was huge and quick. He took another handoff and was busting through the offensive line right toward Luke. Luke ran up to meet him in the hole, but number twelve bulldozed him right into the ground and kept on running down the field, knocking down two other players before he was finally brought down five yards from the goal line. How had he done that? Luke wasn't a small guy, yet he'd been flattened like a pancake!

The crowd went silent. Everyone rose to their feet, going still as the play ended.

It was then that I looked back to where Luke had been tackled. He still hadn't gotten up. He lay flat on his back, not moving.

I grabbed onto Eliana's arm. "Is he okay?" I asked, my voice coming out in a gasp.

"I don't know." She stood on her tiptoes, trying to see over the guy in front of us.

Heart pounding faster than ever before, I squeezed past the people on our row and stumbled down the bleachers, gripping the rail so I didn't topple over.

What was wrong with him? He still hadn't gotten up. He was just lying there on the field, not moving. That wasn't normal. He'd always gotten right back up before.

The coach and the EMTs ran onto the field with a stretcher. Soon they surrounded him, bending down on their knees, checking to see if he was okay. Was he alive? What was happening? He had just gotten hit. Nothing serious could've happened, right?

Luke just lay there for the longest minute of my life. But then finally, finally, he tried to sit up only to be pushed back down by the coach. I pinched my eyes shut, blinking back tears as his dad ran onto the field. A moment later, the EMTs wheeled Luke into the back of the ambulance, his dad climbing in after him.

34

ASHLYN

THE CROWD BUZZED with everyone speculating what was wrong with Luke. My ears flooded with conversations I didn't want to hear, because if everyone around me was talking about Luke being hurt, it meant I hadn't imagined it.

"He broke his back. That's why he wasn't moving," a girl in a black hoodie on the front row said.

"I bet he's paralyzed from the waist down. He's lucky to be alive," the guy beside her added.

"He's probably just faking it," another voice said from behind me.

I couldn't listen to it anymore, so I left the field and drove to the hospital. I needed to know that he was okay.

"CAN I please get the status on Luke Davenport?" I asked the receptionist at the ER department of the Ridgewater hospital. "He was brought here in an ambulance about an hour ago."

"Are you family?" she asked.

I should have known she'd ask that question. Would it be so bad if I lied?

"No, I'm not family. I'm his...friend." At least I hoped he was okay enough that we could become friends again.

"I'm sorry, but I can't give you any information."

I sighed. It had been a long shot anyway.

I walked back to the waiting area and slumped down in a cushioned seat. I was surprised that there weren't any other people here from school. The only other person I recognized was the red-headed woman who had been at the game with Luke's dad.

I grabbed a magazine from a table and tried to distract myself. About thirty minutes later, the door opened and Luke's dad came through. I studied his face and his body language to try and see what I could learn. Was he devastated? Was he just tired? He scrubbed a hand through his graying hair and sighed. I decided he was just tired. Hopefully that meant Luke was okay.

He walked over to the red-headed woman and sank down beside her. I held my breath and perked up my ears, hoping I could gain something from whatever he said to her.

"He's going to be okay," he said, his voice heavy with exhaustion. "He suffered a mild concussion, but the doctor thinks he should make a full recovery. He just needs to take it easy for the next few days."

My body went weak with relief and I wanted to cry. He was okay. Just a mild concussion. Nothing like what I'd feared.

I listened for any other information. His dad just talked about how they would be able to leave in the next little while and he'd be taking him home to get some rest. Then he said something about how he didn't think it would be the best idea for her to be in the car with them.

The woman nodded but looked disappointed at those words. And I tried to imagine what it would be like to be in her shoes.

She probably was a nice lady. She probably really liked Luke's dad. She just happened to get to know him at the wrong time for Luke. But she seemed shaken enough over the whole situation that it made me wonder if she might already care about Luke too. And that was a very interesting thought. I knew Luke missed his mom terribly, but maybe it wouldn't be so bad for him to have another woman to love him. He was pretty easy to love, after all.

I LEFT the hospital shortly after hearing the news about Luke. He'd already suffered enough trauma for one night. I didn't want to add any more drama by being there. I still didn't know exactly what our relationship would look like from here on out, since I had no idea what he would want. But I knew that I definitely wanted to change things. It had only taken a few seconds of seeing him there lifeless on the field to realize that he was way more important to me than any of the anger that I'd been holding onto.

In hindsight, it was stupid that I'd gotten so mad about him being British Boy. In the grand scheme of things, was it really that big of a deal that he'd used a fake accent on me? He told me himself in the Chemistry lab, right after we kissed the first time, that he had only started this whole thing because he didn't think I would have wanted him otherwise. And then, of course, being the fool that I am, I went and proved him right. As soon as I found out that he was British Boy I didn't want him anymore.

But I did want him. I wanted him so badly that my chest felt like it was collapsing just thinking about him.

Why had I deleted all the messages he had sent me? At least with those I could pretend that things might somehow turn out okay between us. That somehow he could forgive my stupidity.

I was awake for much of the night, tossing and turning,

because my brain wouldn't shut off. We were supposed to practice our dance in the morning, but with this new turn of events I was sure Luke would be out of the competition. Looked like I'd gotten what I wanted after all.

I waited clear until one p.m. before driving over to Luke's house with a pot of chicken noodle soup. My mom had the best recipe I'd ever tasted, so I hoped it might help cheer him up.

There was a bunch of cars parked outside his house when I arrived. Apparently, I wasn't the only one with the idea to visit him. But I grabbed my pot of soup and knocked anyway.

His dad greeted me at the door and invited me into the house. Several of Luke's football buddies were sitting in the living room along with a few of the cheerleaders as well. Jake, Kellen, and Denton sat on the couch. The girls sat on the loveseat. And Luke rested on a recliner that must've been brought into the room just for his recovery. I hadn't seen it in there when we'd practiced before. The blinds were closed and the lights turned off, so it was pretty dim. I imagined it was like that for his recovery or something.

A hush fell over the room once they noticed me. My face flushed as I handed the pot of soup to Luke's dad.

"I thought he might like this," I said to him in a low voice, hoping the others wouldn't overhear.

He took the pot from my hands and smiled gratefully, and I noticed he had the same eyes as Luke. "It's been a long time since we've had a good home-cooked meal. Thank you, Ashlyn."

I nodded, still not sure what I was going to do next. I hadn't planned on there being so many people here when I tried to talk to Luke. But I should have known; he was a well-liked guy at school.

Luke's dad nodded toward the living room. "Go ahead and have a seat. I'm sure Luke will be happy to see you."

I found an empty chair next to the head cheerleader.

"Hi, Luke," I said, tucking some hair behind my ear when everyone kept staring at me.

"Hey," was all he said before turning his attention back to the conversation with his friends. I wanted to turn invisible and disappear from the room. Why did I think that he'd want to see me? Of course he didn't want to see me, not after the way I'd treated him this past week. I shouldn't have come at all. This was completely awkward.

I just sat there for the next thirty minutes, quietly listening to his friends talk. Luke was pretty quiet too, but I figured a lot of that was because of the concussion. And the more I watched him, the more I noticed that he kept drifting off to sleep as everyone conversed around him.

Eventually, his dad came back into the room to tell us that we needed to go so Luke could get some rest. I took my time standing, hoping to get a moment alone with him before leaving. His buddies patted him on the shoulder and told him to get better soon. The girls gave him hugs and told him they were happy that he was okay. I had no idea what I'd do when my turn came. But finally, the room was empty, leaving Luke and me alone for a moment.

"How are you feeling?" I asked when he slid his drowsy gaze to me.

"Honestly?"

I nodded. "Of course."

"I feel like I got ran over by a bus."

"Well, you pretty much did."

His lip quirked up into a small smile, which put me more at ease than anything else had all day. If he was still able to joke around, he was going to be okay.

"If you came over to practice our waltz, I'm sorry to say that the doctor banned me from it."

"I pretty much figured that. And don't worry about it. I'll talk to Max."

"Thanks," he said. "But just so you know, I totally didn't try to get run over just to get out of the dance. This was a true accident."

I gave him an understanding smile. "I know. You just work on getting yourself better. And I'll see you at school later this week."

I wanted to hug him, but my body didn't seem to remember how. Instead, I wrung my hands in front of me before finally making my awkward escape out the door.

35

LUKE

WHEN I CAME down for breakfast Monday morning, Dad was sitting at the bar with his laptop open in front of him.

"How's your head feeling today?" he asked.

"A bit of a headache, but better."

I couldn't remember what happened in the moments before I received my concussion, and not much of what happened the next day either. That's the fun thing with brain injuries, I guess. My dad reminded me that I had a lot of visitors come over and that Ashlyn was one of them. She didn't come back after the first day though, which had me worried that maybe I hadn't been very welcoming to her. But I hoped when I went back to school that she'd forgive anything I might've said or done and let me blame it on my low-functioning brain.

I glanced at the clock on the wall and frowned at my dad. "What are you still doing here? Weren't you supposed to be at work an hour ago?"

He shook his head. "I took the day off."

I almost tripped. "You took the day off?" He barely took sick days, and that was only when he was throwing up.

He closed his laptop. "I wanted to be here for you if you needed me."

I grabbed a bowl from the cupboard, still not sure what to make of this. "You don't have to do that. I'm okay on my own. I know how important work is to you."

He looked at me pointedly. "You're important to me, too. I know I haven't done the best job of showing you that in the past, but I want to change things. We need to start acting like a family."

A family of two, since mom was gone and Alec was half a world away.

I pulled a gallon of milk out of the fridge and poured myself a bowl of granola. "Would this *acting like a family* include Amy?"

I glanced at him to see his reaction. His face didn't give much away, but he seemed to be thinking my remark over.

I dug into my bowl of oatmeal, nuts, and raisins. My dad had found a brand of old-fashioned type granola at the grocery store last month that was similar to my mom's, but it still wasn't quite as good. It didn't have enough raisins in it or something.

"About Amy," he said after a minute. "I'm really sorry that I went about introducing her the wrong way. It's not something I ever planned on doing, so I'm just fumbling my way around." He sighed and looked at me more carefully, like he was trying to see into my soul. "Do you remember what Mom told us over and over during those last months with her?"

I thought about it and shrugged. "I don't know. She said a lot of things."

His gaze softened. "She didn't want her death to be the reason for us to stop living. She wanted us to be happy."

"And Amy makes you happy?" I said bitterly.

"Yes, actually, she does. I know the timing was terrible for you, and I still have to tell your brother about it, but to me, she feels like an angel. She came to me at my darkest hour and rescued me."

I scowled into my bowl, not wanting to look at him. I didn't want to have this conversation. He'd betrayed my mom. She'd only been gone for a couple of months before he decided their twenty-five-year marriage was recyclable.

"I hadn't planned to tell you this," he continued. "But about a month and a half after your mom died, I hit a really low point. I got to where I didn't see a point in living anymore. It just hurt too much to be without her. The months and years stretched ahead of me in an infinity of pain that I didn't want to face. I figured you were pretty much an adult. You didn't need me anymore. Alec had been out of the house for a couple of years and barely saw the need to talk to me much, anyway."

My throat constricted. I didn't like the way this was going. I didn't know if I should be hearing this, not from my dad.

He swallowed. "I had it all planned. I was going to stay late at work, like I always did. I figured it would be better for someone to discover me there the next morning, instead of having you find me. I had a bunch of sleeping pills that I'd been using to help me sleep since your mom died. I could just swallow a bottle of those and never have to wake up. Never have to feel the pain of living without your mom again."

Tears pricked behind my eyes. I could barely believe what I was hearing. My dad had been the strong one. He wasn't the weak person who had panic attacks. He'd been able to move on like nothing had ever happened.

"I went into my office and was holding the bottle in my hands when I heard your mother's voice. She said, 'Don't you dare do that, Brady. Don't you dare throw away the time we all wish I'd have more of. Don't you dare take away the only parent our boys have.'"

Chills ran down my back. I could hear my mom's sweet, smooth voice in my mind. The tears spilled out, and when I looked at my dad's face, his eyes were wet, too.

"It was then that I heard someone else." His voice shook. "It was Amy. She had come back to the office, feeling like she needed to check on me for some reason. She found me curled up on my office floor, a broken man, and I knew your mom had sent her to me. She wanted to make sure you weren't left here alone. Wanted to make sure I didn't ruin everything forever."

Emotion had built up in my throat. I swallowed it down to speak. "That's why you called her your angel?"

He nodded and wiped at his eye. "She and your mother are my angels. Your mom is my angel in heaven. Amy is my angel on earth. She talked me down from the cliff. You see, her husband died in a plane crash a few years ago, so she understood what I was going through. She helped me find the strength to live when I didn't think I had any more to find. She became a good friend, and I really do think your mom sent her to be with me. She knew we needed someone else to love us, and Amy does."

My heart wanted to soften at his words, but they didn't make any sense. "Amy doesn't even know me."

"I've told her all about you. And when I didn't think I could bear to go to your football games without your mom there, worried I'd break down when I didn't hear her yelling at the refs, Amy went for me."

"Amy went to my games?" How many bombshells was he going to drop this morning?

He nodded. "She sent me video clips of your different plays so I could watch them as I listened to the games from the car on the radio."

"You were in the parking lot for all my games?"

He nodded. "Every single one. I'm so sorry I never came out until last week." His eyes were wide and vulnerable. "I'm sorry I've been so weak. I haven't been there for you like I needed to. But I'm really hoping this can be a turning point for us. I've been selfish, only thinking about myself and my pain. I neglected the most important person I have in my life right now."

I looked down at my cereal, my jaw working as I processed everything that he'd said to me over the past few minutes. My dad was just as broken as me. He hadn't moved on from my mom—if anything, he'd taken it harder. We just had different ways of coping with the pain.

Dad got up, the bar stool scraping across the tile. And before I could think, he gave me a hug. We clung to each other, weeping like big babies. I had hated him for so many months, but now I could feel part of my heart healing.

After we composed ourselves once more, I sat back down, thinking. I knew I needed to make a peace offering as well.

"Do you think we could try that dinner with Amy again?" I sighed, not believing what I was saying. "I think I'd like to get to know her better."

He smiled, probably the first smile I'd seen him wear since Mom died. "I think we can arrange that."

MY DAD and I spent the next two days together, watching football and talking about some of our favorite memories of Mom. We planned to take a trip to Yellowstone, one of her favorite places on earth, when my brother had his leave in a few months. Our relationship still wasn't perfect, and we both had a lot of healing to do, but things were getting better—and "getting better" was an improvement from where we'd been a week ago.

There was a knock on our front door Wednesday evening. The steady stream of visitors had become a lot less steady, so I had no idea who might be here. But I hoped it was Ashlyn.

Instead, I found Noah on the front porch with his hands shoved in his pockets.

For a second, I wondered if I was hallucinating or something, another side effect of my concussion, but when he grunted and asked if he could talk to me for a minute I decided he must be real enough.

We sat in my living room. He looked around the photos on the wall before speaking. "You're probably wondering why I'm here," he said.

I nodded. "Yeah, can't say that I expected to find you here."

"I'm surprised myself." He cleared his throat. "But I've been meaning to talk to you for the last few days. And since you're too wimpy to show up at school, I figured I'd come over." His lips lifted into a teasing smile.

"Totally wimpy." I shook my head and smiled despite myself.

He rubbed his hand along his pant leg, like he was trying to get up the nerve to say something to me. If he was going to gloat about getting Ashlyn back from me, I might just have to disobey the doctor's orders and get physical.

He swallowed. "I think there might have been a little misunderstanding about why I was at Ashlyn's house last weekend."

"Misunderstanding?"

"I don't really want to go into the details of why I was there. But there's nothing going on between us. She was just helping me out."

Helping him out? That really didn't tell me anything. You could help people out in a lot of different ways.

He continued, "I got into a fight and she helped bandage me up. I fell asleep on her bed, but when I woke up she was sleeping in a chair. So no, nothing happened. And from what I've noticed of her since then, I'm pretty sure she misses you. Though the verdict is still out on whether she should choose you over someone as awesome as me." He grinned. I still didn't like the guy, but I had to hand it to him: it was a stand-up move to tell me this even though I was pretty sure he still had feelings for Ashlyn.

But I couldn't blame him—Ashlyn was a hard girl to get over. Probably impossible to get over.

"Thanks for telling me that, Noah. I appreciate it." We both stood, and I walked him back to the door, since he seemed to have said everything he needed to.

He turned back to me just before leaving. "But don't think for a second that just because I'm letting you have Ashlyn that I'm gonna go easier on you during practice."

I chuckled. "I wouldn't have it any other way."

36

ASHLYN

"ASHLYN, you're wanted at the door." Macey called to me Thursday evening when I was finishing up dinner.

When she came back to find me, I whispered, "Who is it?"

"It's Luke."

A field of butterflies flooded my stomach. "Luke? As in...?"

She nodded, grinning mischievously. "As in, major hottie who can use a British accent anytime you want to go weak at the knees."

I rolled my eyes and gently shoved her arm. But before going into the entryway, I checked myself using my phone's camera app real quick to make sure I looked okay, especially because I'd just gotten home from my dance practice. Why didn't he come over yesterday instead, when I'd been looking more alluring? But there was no time to fix that now, so I took a deep breath and walked to the front door.

He was leaning against the railing when I spotted him through the opening in the doorway. And I wanted to run up the stairs and get an instant makeover, because he looked amazing.

Like, take-my-breath-away good. He stood tall when he heard my footsteps.

"Hey, Luke." I waved, hoping I could play off how nervous and intimidated I was to see him. Things hadn't exactly gone well the last few times we'd seen each other. Part of me hoped that maybe his concussion had magically made him forget all the stupid things I'd said and done over the past weeks.

He held up the stainless-steel stock pot I'd taken to his house on Saturday. "I thought your mom might want this back."

I took it from him, our hands touching in the exchange, warmth flickering to where our fingers had met. "Thank you." I felt my cheeks heat.

He nodded. "The soup was great."

We stood there staring at each other awkwardly for a few seconds before my brain kicked in. "D-do you want to come in?"

He rocked forward on his toes. "Actually, I was wondering if you'd like to go on a walk with me."

"A walk?" I'd never been asked to go on a walk with a guy in my entire life. My pulse raced with anticipation as I thought of all the reasons why he'd want to go for a walk.

When I was quiet for too long, he said, "I want to talk to you, if you're not too busy."

"I'm not too busy," I blurted out.

He smiled, and my blush deepened. I'd missed his smile so much!

"Let me put this in the kitchen and grab a jacket. I'll be right back."

"Okay." He leaned back against the railing, making himself comfortable.

I zoomed into the kitchen and set the pot on the counter. I could put it away later. Then I rushed up the stairs, taking two at a time, and sped straight to my bathroom.

I inspected my hair in the mirror. My messy bun would not

do for a walk—an evening stroll—with Luke. I ran my brush through it a few times until it was smooth, and then quickly brushed my teeth, just in case.

Once I was more presentable and had lightly spritzed myself with my "special date" perfume, I grabbed my pink jacket and hurried back downstairs.

Luke grinned when he saw me, and I could be wrong but there was a hint of admiration in his gaze.

"Which way do you want to go?" I asked, somewhat breathless, and not just because I'd sprinted around the house.

"Let's go that way." He pointed in the direction of the park.

He buttoned up his letterman jacket and started down the path. The sun was beginning to set, and there was a slight breeze in the crisp fall air.

"Did you go watch the competition on Saturday?" he asked when we turned onto the main sidewalk.

I nodded. "Yeah. It was really good. Kelsie and Stan won, of course."

"Of course," he said. "But that's probably only because we had to drop out. I'm still sorry about that, by the way. I know how much you love dancing."

"It's okay. I'm just glad you seem to be doing better. How are you feeling, anyway?"

He shrugged. "Much better. My headaches stopped a couple of days ago, and I don't think my brain got messed up too much."

"That's good." I looked down, watching my feet, one foot stepping in front of the other. "I was really worried about you. I was so relieved when I overheard your dad tell that red-headed woman that you were going to be okay."

"When were you around Amy and my dad?"

I tucked some hair behind my ear. "I followed the ambulance to the hospital." I watched him carefully, gauging his reaction to see how much that freaked him out.

His eyes widened for a second, but then he smiled gently. As if he liked that I'd gone there. "You were at the hospital?"

"I had to know that you were okay. I was so worried." Visions of him being hauled into an ambulance and driving away pushed themselves into my mind.

His gaze softened, and I knew that he understood the depth of my feelings. They had to be written all over my face.

"I'm glad I'm okay, too. And it means a lot that you came to the hospital. I definitely didn't deserve it after everything I'd done."

We walked in silence for a while, each lost in our own thoughts. A couple of cars drove past, the only distractions on this quiet evening.

It was so strange that things could change so quickly. At the beginning of the school year, we barely knew each other. Our only interactions had been in a stupid pranking war. And now, I couldn't think of another human on the entire planet that I'd rather be with. I liked him so much. Maybe was even starting to fall in love with him... Could I hope that he might be feeling the same things? After everything?

We made it to the park, and he turned onto the sidewalk that led to the old, white gazebo. We stepped into it and leaned against the railing, taking in our surroundings. The park was all but deserted on this autumn evening. The leaves had changed colors and were starting to fall from their branches, leaving the grass covered with splashes of yellow, brown, and red. I loved that we had seasons to remind us that the world was still spinning and time kept moving on. Nothing ever stayed the same, but maybe that was a good thing. I would hate to be the same person I was before getting to know Luke.

I'd learned a lot about myself in the past few weeks, and one was that I didn't forgive as easily as I should. I'd let anger and past hurts drive my life way too much. Holding a grudge was like drinking poison and waiting for the other person to die. It was stupid and did nothing to help me get into a better spot. I didn't need to stay forever mad at Noah for how he'd treated me. Yes, he hadn't been a very good boyfriend, and I was glad I'd gotten out when I had, but he was dealing with demons of his own. I really hoped he could get past them and be happy.

And if I could forgive Noah, there was absolutely no reason why I should have been so upset at Luke. It was embarrassing to think about how badly I'd overreacted.

"I'm sorry that I got so mad when I found out you were British Boy." I sighed, turning around so I was facing him. "I pretty much proved you right in why you didn't want to tell me."

He shook his head. "Don't be. I shouldn't have started it in the first place. It just sort of happened, and then before I knew it, it was out of control."

"I'm surprised at how well you managed it. You must be a genius to have come up with it all."

He laughed. "Genius or imbecile. Pretty sure it's one of those."

"Did you know it was me from the very first day?"

He nodded, his brown eyes meeting mine in the filtered sunlight, making my heart stutter. "I didn't know from the moment you tripped over my huge feet and we bonked heads, but, yeah, once I heard you laugh, I knew it was you. I might have had a tiny crush on you last year."

"Really?" My jaw dropped. Luke had liked me that long ago? I felt breathless at the thought.

"Yeah, why else do you think I picked you for my pranks? I was totally flirting with you."

I leaned my head back and laughed. "You have an interesting way of showing that you like someone."

He tilted his head to the side and shrugged. "Then how would you suggest I let a certain person know that I like her?"

My cheeks heated. I'd walked right into that, hadn't I?

I bit my lip as I thought about it. "I can think of a couple of ways."

"You can?" He arched an eyebrow and stepped closer. "And what's one of those ways?"

"Holding hands is usually a good sign."

He immediately reached over and clasped my hand in his, interlocking our fingers. Warmth spread its way up my arm. I'd missed being so close to him. Touching him.

"Like this?" he asked, lifting our hands and kissing the back of mine.

I couldn't keep from smiling wider as I watched him. "That's one way to do it."

He squeezed my hand, and I returned the gesture. I would be completely content just holding his hand forever.

"What's another way to let a girl know that I'm into her?"

Into her. He made those two words sound way too good.

Maybe holding his hand wasn't quite enough after all.

"Hugs are usually good." I shrugged, hoping to come off nonchalant.

"Yeah?" He stepped closer, tilting his head low so I could look straight into his eyes. The way he was studying me made my stomach flip. His gaze seemed to trace over my face. He was sooo attractive. I couldn't handle it.

I swallowed. "Yep. Hugs are the best."

"Well then," he said in a low, provocative voice. "I think I might just have to hug you."

He closed the distance between us and pulled me into his arms. I melted into him, letting his strong embrace envelop me with warmth. I sighed. Luke's hugs were the best. I nuzzled my face into his neck, breathing in his fresh, clean scent.

"You smell much better than you did as British Boy that first time we kissed," I said, breathing him in again.

His chest rumbled as he chuckled. "I'm glad you think so. That 'old-man' scent you accused me of having was my dad's cologne. I had to disguise myself somehow."

I slapped his shoulder gently and pulled away so I could see his face. "I can't believe you did that!"

He grinned, his eyes smiling. "Like we established earlier, I was out of my mind desperate not to get caught."

"Well, I'm happy to know that all the things I liked about British Boy are part of you. Knowing the whole Luke is pretty incredible."

"It sounds like we'd make a great couple then, since you're the most amazing girl I've ever met."

My heart thudded in my chest at his words. No one had ever made me feel this way before. I felt light, like I could float into the air and touch the sun.

He leaned his forehead against mine and spoke in a quiet voice. "Are there any other things a guy should do to let a girl know that he likes her?"

"How about you try figuring the last one out yourself?"

And with those words, he didn't hesitate to close the gap between our lips. His mouth pressed against mine, starting out slow and searching, like he had all the time in the world. He leaned his tall body against me, trapping me between him and the gazebo's railing. I reveled in the feeling. I loved being so close to him—my body craved it. I didn't want there to be any space between us. We'd already had too much of that over the past weeks.

"I think I more than like you, Ashlyn." His voice was low and seductive against my lips, sending shivers tingling down my spine. "Is this what I'm supposed to do when I more than like you?"

"Yes." I sighed, and he captured my lips between his again. Time stopped. It was like the earth stopped spinning, the moon stopped rising, and the leaves stopped falling. I wanted to bottle up this moment and keep it with me forever. Nothing could top this.

I let my hands travel from where they rested around his waist, feeling his strong muscular torso, moving up until my fingers tangled in his soft hair. He let out a low growl, causing me to smile against his lips.

"I like you so much," I told him, my heart beating so fast and hard in my chest I was sure he could feel it. "Probably more than like you."

His arms tightened around my waist and I let myself get lost in the moment. Being with Luke was magical, and I couldn't wait to let our "more than like" turn into love. In all my life, no moment had ever felt as perfect as this. Luke was mine and I was his, and everything was right in my world.

EPILOGUE

LUKE

"DID you see that they put the posters up for the Sweethearts Ball?" Ashlyn asked me as we walked to her locker before school one morning. We'd been dating for three spectacular months, and I had never been happier than I was now. Ashlyn had changed me. Before her, I had been a lost soul, wandering through life not knowing where to go. But meeting her that one day in the Chemistry lab had changed everything for me. My life had new purpose. She had catapulted me toward a future that I was excited about, instead of dreading.

"Yeah, I saw the posters. They look pretty good, huh?" I asked, pretending like I didn't know what she was trying to hint at.

"They do look nice. The dance sounds like it'll be fun."

I shrugged. "I guess, if you're into that whole dancing thing."

"Which I obviously am." She shook her head. "I'm really hoping to go with this year's All-State Linebacker. Did you hear that he got a scholarship to play football at Cortland State next year?"

I gasped, feigning surprise. I loved how proud she was of me. "He must be a pretty big deal."

"He totally is. Anyway, I can't imagine a better dance partner. In fact, if I went with him, I'd probably try to request our favorite waltz, *A Thousand Years*."

"Don't let him hear you say that. You might scare him away."

She smiled, and I wanted to kiss her. She was breathtaking when she was smiling at me.

We made it to her locker, and I held my breath as she opened it.

"When did you put this here?" she asked, taking out the note I'd hid in there while she was in drill practice this morning.

"Open it," I said.

She unfolded the paper and read the words "Meet me there at lunch" written in permanent marker in my own messy scrawl.

"Meet you where?" She looked up at me with question and anticipation in her eyes.

"You'll figure it out." I winked and kissed her on the cheek. "But for now, we better get to class."

I LEFT class early so I could make it to the Chemistry lab before Ashlyn did. I knew I shouldn't be nervous, since she'd practically told me she wanted me to do this, but my stomach was still twisted up in knots because I wanted this to be perfect.

I stepped into the dark lab room, opting to leave the lights off for tradition's sake. Ashlyn could turn them on when she got here.

The door creaked open a few minutes later, light streaming in through the small crack in the door.

"Is anyone in here?" Ashlyn's voice cut through the air.

I smiled, remembering all the times she'd done that very thing before. "Yes. I'm in here." My palms started to sweat. I really hoped she'd like this.

She stepped inside and shut the door behind her, the room instantly going pitch black.

"You can turn on the light," I said, using my British accent.

She laughed. "Okay. Good."

I heard her feel around the wall for a moment before the lights flicked on.

I watched her face for the reaction I'd hoped she'd have. She didn't disappoint. Her mouth hung open, and she gasped at the poster I'd stuck on the wall.

DATE WANTED!

For: Luke Davenport at the Sweethearts Ball.
Who: You, Ashlyn Brooks, of course!
Why: I'll list a few of the many, many reasons, below.

"I can't believe you did this." Ashlyn turned to me, the joy in her face making my heart swell.

She moved closer to the poster, running her fingers over the photo I'd put on it—a selfie of us together at the Football State Championship game.

"I see your neighbor was too busy to draw a picture for you this time. How did you do this?" she asked, stepping back to take in the whole thing.

"I've been planning it for months." I moved to stand behind her, wrapping my arms around her waist and pulling her against my chest. "I know you can read it yourself, but is it okay if I read my reasons to you?"

She pressed her lips into a huge grin and nodded. "I'd love that."

I leaned my chin on her shoulder and read the words I'd written on the flyer, using my own voice instead of my British accent. "Number ten: I love how obsessed you are with dance. You almost make me like it, too."

She laughed, and my chest felt light.

"Number nine: You make life exciting and always keep me on my toes. Number eight: When I'm with you, I can handle anything."

"The feeling is mutual," she interrupted.

I gave her a squeeze before continuing. "Number seven: You make me laugh all the time. Number six: You love me despite my imperfections."

"What imperfections?"

I shook my head and continued, "Number five: You make me happier than I've ever been. Number four: Your hugs are amazing. Number three: You're the most beautiful person I've ever met. Inside and out. Number two: You make me want to be a better man. And number one..."

"You left number one blank?" She turned in my arms to face me.

"Noticed that, did you?"

"Couldn't think of a number one?" She raised her eyebrows, challenging me in the way that I loved.

"I wanted to tell it to you instead of reading it."

She bit her lip, and the urge to kiss her almost beat out my resolve to tell her my number one thing. But no, I needed to hold off. I could kiss her afterward. I *would* kiss her afterward.

I lowered my voice and leaned my forehead against hers as I said my next words. "The number one reason why I want to go to the dance with you is because I love you, Ashlyn. And I love us."

She looked at me through her lashes, a contented smile on her lips. "I love you, too, Luke. And of course, I'll go with you," she whispered before taking my face in her hands and pulling my lips to hers.

She kissed me, and I knew I could never grow tired of this.

When we separated, she looked up at me with those beautiful blue eyes of hers. "Did you mean all those things you said?"

I nodded and kissed her once more. "Every single word."

READ THE NEXT BOOK IN THIS SERIES:
DON'T FORGET ME
ELIANA AND JESS'S STORY

Sparks are flying between these best friends.
Could a practice kiss change everything?

Seventeen-year-old Eliana Costa has never kissed a guy. Her best guy friend, Jess, is more than willing to help her out. He has plenty of experience, since he finds a new girlfriend every other week. But when a practice kiss brings on feelings Eliana hadn't bargained for, her already messy life is thrown into a new level of chaos.

Life is already more than she can handle after her dad's disappearance. Eliana worries that if she admits her feelings to Jess, she just might lose her best friend. And right now, a best friend is all she needs. But when another girl tries to date Jess, Eliana is forced to decide if taking a chance on love is worth the risk.

Grab your copy today!

ALSO BY JUDY CORRY

Ridgewater High Series:

Meet Me There (Ashlyn and Luke)

Don't Forget Me (Eliana and Jess)

It Was Always You (Lexi and Noah)

My Second Chance (Juliette and Easton)

My Mistletoe Mix-Up (Raven and Logan)

Forever Yours (Alyssa and Jace)

Protect My Heart (Emma and Arie)

The Billionaire Bachelor (Kate and Drew)

Kissing The Boy Next Door (Wes and Lauren)

Coming Summer 2019
Jace and Alyssa's story.

Her crush is back.
Too bad she's dating his best friend.

Join Judy's VIP Reader's Club to be notified when it's released.
http://www.subscribepage.com/judycorry

ACKNOWLEDGMENTS

I kind of can't believe that I'm here again! But I know it wouldn't be possible without some pretty amazing people in my life. So this is for them...

First off, I need thank my wonderful husband, Jared, for supporting me in this writing dream of mine, for holding down the fort at times so I could meet my crazy deadlines, and then for being a great listening ear when I was stuck—which happened after almost every chapter!

Thanks to James, Janelle, Jonah, and Jade for letting me talk about my books and characters with you. I love how excited you were about Ashlyn and Luke's story and how you make me feel like the coolest author mom in the world.

To my critique partners—Anne-Marie Meyer, Michelle Pennington, Victorine Lieske, Kiersten Marquet, Jenny Rabe, Paige Edwards, and Cassie Shiels. Without your amazing insights and support, I never would have figured this story out!

To my beta-readers whose feedback is invaluable: Jami Lyn Niles, Michelle Carter, Brookie Cowles, Julie L. Spencer, Cathy

Woolsey, and Kristin Clove. Thank you for taking a chance on another book!

To my dance experts: Taylor Beagley and Brittney Corry.

To Precy Larkins, for being my rock star editor. You are amazing at helping my books get to the next level!

To my cover designer, Victorine E. Lieske, for once again making a gorgeous cover!

Thank you to all my family and friends for your love and support through this crazy adventure of mine. I couldn't do it without you.

Thank you to the members of my online writing community who have been so willing to share your wisdom and help make this publishing adventure so much less daunting than it would have been on my own.

I'm especially thankful to my Heavenly Father for the inspiration and "aha" moments. Sometimes I like to think that I'm in charge of my stories, but I'm pretty sure I'm not.

ABOUT THE AUTHOR

Judy Corry has been addicted to love stories for as long as she can remember. She reads and writes YA and Clean Romance because she can't get enough of the feeling of falling in love. She graduated from Southern Utah University with a degree in Family Life and Human Development and loves to weave what she learned about the human experience into her stories. She believes in swoon-worthy kisses and happily ever afters.

Judy met her soul mate while in high school, and married him a few years later. She and her husband are raising four beautiful and crazy children in Southern Utah.

Made in the USA
Las Vegas, NV
04 December 2020

12019855R00152